"Hey, cowboy. Did y[...] something?"

Seated on the passenger side with Lady in her lap, Lauren's daughter grinned and waved.

If a heart could burst with happiness, Rob's would do so right now. Exiting the truck, he crossed the highway to speak to Lauren.

"Thanks for bringing her back. Don't know what I'm gonna do with that little gal." He could see Lauren's guarded expression. After his unfair accusations when they met, he didn't blame her. "Where did you find her?"

"We found her curled up outside our apartment door. Want to take her now? Or I can leave her at the ranch."

"We'll take her. Can you fit the kids in your car? Don't want them to be late to Sunday school."

The shuffle of bodies on the side of the road was more chaotic than it should have been, with each of his kids insisting on welcoming Lady back and Lady trying to wriggle free and get back to Zoey. In the truck, Mom finally had Lady in hand.

"Well, that's something." Mom petted Lady.

"What's something?"

"You just sent your kids off with a woman who, three months ago, you had no use for." She grinned. "Are we seeing a little, um, *romance* developing?"

Award-winning author **Louise M. Gouge** writes historical and contemporary fiction romances. She received the prestigious Inspirational Readers' Choice Award in 2005 and was a finalist in 2011, 2015, 2016 and 2017; was a finalist in the 2012 Laurel Wreath contest; and was a 2023 Selah Award finalist. She taught English and humanities at Valencia College for sixteen and a half years and has written twenty-eight novels, eighteen of which were published under Harlequin's Love Inspired imprint. Contact Louise at louisemgougeauthor.blogspot.com, Facebook.com/louisemgougeauthor and on X, @louisemgouge.

Books by Louise M. Gouge

Love Inspired

Safe Haven Ranch

K-9 Companions

A Faithful Guardian

Love Inspired Historical

Finding Her Frontier Family
Finding Her Frontier Home

Four Stones Ranch

Cowboy to the Rescue
Cowboy Seeks a Bride
Cowgirl for Keeps
Cowgirl Under the Mistletoe
Cowboy Homecoming
Cowboy Lawman's Christmas Reunion

Visit the Author Profile page at LoveInspired.com for more titles.

A FAITHFUL GUARDIAN

LOUISE M. GOUGE

LOVE INSPIRED
INSPIRATIONAL ROMANCE

LOVE INSPIRED®

INSPIRATIONAL ROMANCE

ISBN-13: 978-1-335-93696-7

Recycling programs
for this product may
not exist in your area.

A Faithful Guardian

Love Inspired
22 Adelaide St. West, 41st Floor
Toronto, Ontario M5H 4E3, Canada
www.LoveInspired.com

Printed in Lithuania

MIX
Paper | Supporting
responsible forestry
FSC® C021394

There is a friend that sticketh closer than a brother.
—*Proverbs* 18:24

My special thanks go to my wonderful agent, Tamela Hancock Murray, and to my fabulous editor, Shana Asaro. Thank you for all that you do.

Thanks to my beloved great-niece, Elizabeth Chelsey Lawrence, for providing research about cerebral palsy from her youngest son Nikholas's life experiences so I could accurately portray my character Zoey. Thanks to Elizabeth's daughter Clementine for letting me name a character after her. Thanks also to my beloved granddaughter Emmy Santiago Halaby, who gave me permission to use her real-life seizure episodes to further develop Zoey's story. I pray I was faithful to each of you in this book.

Finally, as with all of my stories, this book is dedicated to my beloved husband, David, my one and only love, who encouraged me to write the stories of my heart and continued to encourage me throughout my writing career. David, I will always love you and miss you.

Chapter One

Robert Mattson slammed on the brakes, then steered his brand-new RAM 3500 into the first empty parking space at the edge of Riverton Park, his eyes laser focused on two women at a picnic table. The dog they were playing with was his cow-herding border collie, Lady, no doubt about it, with her black face and coat and distinctive white heart-shape mark on her chest. How could they dare to bring his stolen dog out in public? He'd demand an answer right before he had them arrested for the theft.

"Siri, call Rex Blake," he ordered. "Hey, Rex," he said when the sheriff answered. "Listen, I found Lady." Pause. "She's with two women at Riverton Park. Can you come over and make the arrest? Great. Thanks." He disconnected the call, shut off the motor and climbed out of his truck, making sure to lock the door, something he'd been doubly careful to do since Lady went missing eight months ago. The sheriff's office was right around the corner, so Rex should be here pretty quick.

The mid-August sunshine bore down on his head, so he put on his weathered Stetson and pulled in a deep breath of fresh air scented with the fragrance of newly mown grass, then moved toward the women to face this unpleasant situation. Several folks waved to him from their picnic tables or Frisbee games. He waved back, mindful that he needed to be careful how he approached these thieves. As he'd learned early in his forty-two years, folks around here looked up to the Mattsons as leaders of the community. As much as he wanted to vent his anger at the women, he needed to set a good example of how to handle an unpleasant and *criminal* situation.

The closer he got to the pair, the more he could see they didn't fit the expected profile for dog thieves. The older woman, maybe in her thirties, was vaguely familiar, and the younger one was just a girl, probably close in age to his own twins' fifteen years. Her jerking movements as she tossed the ball for Lady to fetch, along with her broken laughter when the dog chased it, suggested some sort of disability.

Rob huffed out a long breath. Perfect. Just perfect. His family had always been allies for those with disabilities, so he'd have to be twice as careful not to make a scene.

He approached their picnic table and shoved his Stetson back from his forehead.

"Mornin', ma'am." He aimed a slight smile toward the woman, whose back was now turned, hoping to catch her off guard once she faced him.

"Yes?" She turned around and looked up at him, her pretty face the picture of innocence.

Now who was caught off guard? She wasn't just pretty. She was gorgeous, and her rose-scented perfume wafted up to engage his senses. For some ridiculous reason, his pulse kicked up. Any other time, Rob would have backed off. He had a built-in radar to protect himself from females. Ever since he was a boy, his beloved Jordyn had been his shield against women who regarded his status as the Mattsons' primary heir a prize to grasp at. Since Jordyn's death in a riding accident four years ago had left him a widower, females had swarmed around him like bees, so Rob had been forced to create his own shield, which included keeping his distance and not trusting their motives.

"Did you want something, Mr. Mattson?" The woman gave him a half smile.

How long had he stared at her? And she knew his name. No surprise there because everybody knew the Mattsons. Heat rushed up his neck. He turned his attention to the dog, dug a dog biscuit out of his pocket and crouched down.

"Here, Lady. Come here, girl."

Lady tilted her head and gave him a puzzled look before trotting over to accept the treat. He ruffled her fur and stroked her back and sides, dismayed to feel her protruding ribs. Lady finished the treat, then licked his hand. "That's my girl."

"You know her?" The woman's tone held no guilt.

"Mom?" The girl stepped closer, her ball in hand, a worried frown on her sweet face.

"It's okay, honey." The woman's maternal smile made her even prettier, if that was possible. "Well, Mr. Mattson, you seem to know our Daisy, and she seems to know you."

"She should." Rob stood and towered over her. Unlike most folks, who were awed by his six-foot-three-inch height, she barely tracked his movement with her eyes. "I bought her over two years ago and hand raised her from a puppy. What are you doing with her?"

The question brought an innocent blink from those gray-green eyes. "I… I've been taking care of her." She glanced beyond him with a surprised look.

Rob didn't bother to turn around. Sheriff Rex Blake was a large presence that a man could feel before he saw him.

"Got a problem, Rob?" Rex spoke in his authoritarian lawman voice that no doubt rattled many a lawbreaker's nerves. He watched the woman to see her reaction.

"Yep. Sure do." Rob noticed the woman moving closer to her daughter and putting a protective arm around her. Obviously she couldn't make a run for it. "This woman has my dog I've been looking for since she was stolen last winter."

Rex settled a stern look on the woman, but his expression quickly softened. "Mrs. Parker?"

"Hi, Rex." Her tone sounded guarded. Had she been arrested before?

"Um, Rob?" Rex nudged Rob's arm. "This is Lauren Parker. She's your cousin Will's new paralegal. I met her in his office when I was there on a child custody matter." He chuckled. "You sure you want me to arrest her?"

Rob clenched his jaw so it wouldn't drop open with surprise. Though not too much surprise as he now remembered seeing her across the church's fellowship hall after Will's wedding. In fact, Will had tried to set them up. Fat chance that would happen. Will knew he wasn't interested in dating. "So what are you doing with my dog?" He didn't try to keep the accusing tone from his voice.

"Well, I—"

"I find it interesting—" he refused to listen to her excuse "—that you work for Will and you didn't connect my missing dog to the one you found. We put posters up in every store in town. And don't tell me Will never mentioned the puppies they found out by his place that a DNA test proved were hers. You should have posted a 'found dog' notice."

She stared up at him, annoyance beaming from her eyes. "We found her at a rest stop outside of Santa Fe when we were moving here in May." Her expression softened, enhancing her beauty. "Poor baby was terribly thin and bedraggled...and covered with fleas." She glanced at her daughter, who now knelt beside Lady and held on to her. "We took her to a vet down there and had her checked out, including checking for a chip, but she didn't have one."

"Didn't have a chip? That's a l—" he noticed the startled look in the girl's eyes "—not true. We chip all of our dogs at twelve weeks."

"Well, she didn't have one when we found her." She glared

at Rob. "If she had, we would have brought her to you as soon as we arrived in Riverton. We did the best we could to take care of her and even spent money we couldn't afford to pay the vet for treating her."

Ah, there it was. The money thing. "And no doubt you'll want the reward."

She huffed. "Reward? No, thank you. Taking care of her was the right thing to do. And the joy she's brought us more than makes up for the expense." She gazed at her daughter. "Zoey, this man is Daisy's owner. Remember I told you this might happen."

"Yes, ma'am." Zoey's eyes filled with tears, and she held Lady closer for a few seconds. Then she looked up at Rob, and her heartbroken expression pierced his chest. Her mother's actions were not her fault. "You can take her." A humming sound preceded the girl's words, as though she'd had to take a breath and start her vocal cords before she could speak. She opened her arms to release Lady.

It saddened him to hurt this girl, but he had to focus on his dog and get her back to Bobby as soon as possible so his son could resume her training. He bent down and picked Lady up. She rewarded him by licking his face. After all this time, she still remembered him.

"Okay, Rob." Rex clapped him on the shoulder. "You've got this. See you later."

"Thanks, buddy." He turned away from the women to head back to his truck.

"I have her shot records from that Santa Fe vet," the woman called. "Or I can give you his business card so you can call or email him."

He faced her. "Mrs. Parker, you still haven't told me why you didn't know about my missing dog. I'm sure Will's talked about his pups and their lost mother."

She lifted her chin and glared at him. "We consider it unprofessional to discuss personal matters at the office."

He stared at her for maybe ten seconds. Knowing his sociable cousin Will, he couldn't quite picture that. "Yeah, right." He spun around and strode toward his truck, ignoring Lady's wiggling and whimpering as she looked over his shoulder, no doubt already missing the girl who'd been her best friend all summer. That problem would be fixed after Lady spent enough time with Bobby and remembered where she came from.

Lauren tried to stop shaking but couldn't begin to manage it, even when Zoey sat beside her on the picnic bench and hugged her.

"It's okay, Mom." Zoey laid her head on Lauren's shoulder. "Jesus's got this, so she'll be okay."

As usual, she emitted a little hum before speaking, and her *l*'s came out as *w*'s. Would her fellow students torment her in her new school as they had back in Orlando?

"I know." She patted Zoey's hand. "Jesus has this." She eyed the picnic basket. "You hungry?"

"Not much, but I should eat." Zoey reached for the basket and tugged it closer.

Yes, she should eat. When Zoey went too long without food or water, she was in danger of having a seizure.

Lauren pulled the contents from the basket—sandwiches, chips and iced tea, and left the generic dog kibbles she'd packed. She'd done the best she could for Daisy...Lady, but her money would stretch only so far. No doubt Mr. Mattson would fatten Lady up with one of the healthier, more expensive brands. For that alone, she was glad. For Zoey's broken heart, not so much. But it was too soon to promise a new puppy. Zoey never liked it when she rushed in to try to fix things.

Like right now as she struggled to open the plastic zip bag. But she stuck with it until her uncooperative hands finally separated the sealed sides and removed the sandwich. Lauren watched from the corner of her eye as she opened her own and smelled the delicious aroma of chicken salad. Before she could take a bite, Zoey grasped her hand.

"We gotta say grace, Mom. Dear Jesus, thank You for the food. And thank You that Daisy is going to her new forever home." She laughed softly. "Her new *old* forever home. I know that man will take good care of her."

"Amen." Lauren's eyes burned, but she wouldn't let tears come. Zoey's faith was real and deep and often put her mama to shame. God truly had cared for them these past fifteen years.

Her new job had been a huge blessing and an opportunity to get away from her hometown, where some people still asked her why she'd divorced her husband, as though it had been her fault. Didn't every woman want to be married to Singleton Weatherby Parker? After all, he was the primetime anchor for the local NBC affiliate, handsome beyond words, perfect in his news presentations and a man who managed to skate above controversy without a hint of scandal. Of course those countless admirers didn't know the man off camera. The man who'd rejected his firstborn because of her failure to be perfect and had divorced Lauren because she refused to hide Zoey away in a care home. With the divorce, he'd begrudged the minimum child support the judge ordered. Then he married his pregnant beauty-queen trophy wife, and they now had two perfect children. Good riddance. Except that two years ago, he'd gone to court to request a reduction in his childcare payments, citing financial problems.

Lauren suspected he'd hidden some of his assets, but she couldn't manage the lawyer fees to take him to court, so she'd studied to become a paralegal to combat his scheme. But after earning her certification, she decided to forgo the drama and not to go after him. In fact, she released him from any financial obligation as long as he signed away his parental rights. He was all too happy to do that. Zoey didn't know much about her father, and Lauren deflected her questions as much as she could. She dreaded the day when Zoey demanded better answers.

To make a fresh start, she'd done an online search and applied for several open paralegal jobs. Most wanted applicants with more experience, but somehow she'd snagged a position with Mattson and Mattson, Attorneys at Law, maybe because the two young lawyers were just starting to grow their law office and could only offer a minimal salary. She grabbed the offer like a lifeline.

She and Zoey had packed up and driven west to start their new life, leaving the Sunshine State of Florida for the Land of Sunshine. So far, New Mexico was living up to its reputation, but winter was coming. For the first time in Zoey's life, Lauren would have to buy her a winter coat. That would protect her from the cold, but what would protect her from the challenges she would meet at her new school?

The following Monday, Lauren pulled her car up in front of Riverton High School. "You sure you don't want me to go in with you?" She unclicked her seat belt, ready to get out and walk Zoey into the school building.

"Oh, Mom." Zoey rolled her eyes. "Me and Jesus got this." She managed her typical smirk that always accompanied her deliberate grammar mistakes. She opened her door and scooched to the edge of the seat, carefully planting her feet before grasping the door and pulling herself upright. She slung her backpack over one shoulder, wobbled a bit, righted herself, then shut the door and headed toward the brick building with her familiar halting gait among the other countless students. And she didn't even look back.

Lauren shook her head. Zoey had come a long way in learning to control her uncooperative body, and now she faced this new challenge with her usual courage.

Several students watched her awkward trek across the concrete, but no one said anything, at least not that Lauren could hear.

"Lord, please send her a friend."

In fact, Lauren could use one herself. She'd been on the edge of anxiety since her encounter Saturday with that Mattson person. What a bully, and so much like Singleton. Now, as she drove toward work, her anxiety grew. What would Will and Sam have to say about her encounter with their cousin? Would they believe his not-so-subtle accusation that she'd stolen his valuable dog? Would they fire her?

"Lord, please help. You know my savings are almost gone. I can't start over again." And who would hire her if the Mattson clan turned against her?

Parking in front of the one-story storefront law office, she shook off her dismal thoughts and pasted on her professional smile before entering. Toward the back of the large, open room, newlywed Will sat on the edge of Sam's desk. When she entered, they turned her way, and their serious expressions sent a frisson of alarm through her chest.

"Morning, Lauren." Will's baritone voice sounded much like his older cousin's, and their resemblance was undeniable. "Come on over here for a minute."

She stared at them for a second or two, her heart dropping lower. "Sure."

"Let her put her stuff down, Cuz." Sam had many of the Mattson features as well, except that his hair was light brown instead of black, and his eyes more green than blue.

Lauren set her purse and lunch on her desk, then walked across the room on shaky legs.

"Take a look at this and tell me what you think." Sam

handed her a few sheets of paper, which she couldn't read for the blurriness in her eyes.

She blinked and finally managed to focus on the pages of architectural drawings. "Um, what am I looking at?" Not a pink slip, that was for sure.

"We're trying to decide whether to partition off this room so our clients have more privacy during consultations," Will said, "or find another building already set up that way."

"Or build something new," Sam said. "That'll be pricey, but we're thinking it might be worth the expense in the long run."

"Oh." To her horror, Lauren's voice wobbled.

"Hey, are you okay?" Will stood and grabbed a chair, then helped her sit. "What's going on?"

"Oh," she repeated, scrambling for an intelligent response. "My daughter started at her new school today." She managed a shaky laugh. So much for her claim to Robert Mattson that talking about personal matters was unprofessional.

"Ah," the cousins said in a tenor-baritone duet.

"She'll be okay." Will, ever the optimist, patted her shoulder.

"I know. Thanks." Lauren forced her thoughts away from her unnecessary fears and to the matter at hand. "So, what are the pros and cons of each option?" She fetched a legal pad and pen from her own desk and made columns. "Ideas?"

While they discussed the possibilities, in the back of her mind, Lauren allowed herself some relief. At least for now, her employment wasn't in danger. But how long would it be before Robert Mattson talked to his cousins about Lady and cast doubt on her honesty, a death knell for the job of anyone working in law?

On her way to pick Zoey up from school, Lauren passed that unmistakable huge black Ram truck with Robert Mattson driving the other direction. Even through his dark-tinted window, she could see the handsome cut of his jaw. Unlike her previous encounter with the rancher, this time he was smiling, which greatly enhanced his good looks, much as a smile did for her ex. And, as with her ex, she had no doubt that behind the smile lurked a devious mind that only looked out for himself.

She pulled in behind the other parents' vehicles lined up in front of the school. Most of them were pickup trucks, which made her little eleven-year-old Honda Fit seem even smaller. On the trip from Orlando, they'd had a few scary moments as they traveled alongside semis that seemed intent on squashing them. But she wouldn't trade this comfy little runabout for anything.

"Mom!" Zoey opened the car door and practically jumped inside. "I've got a new friend. *Two* new friends."

"That's awesome, honey." *And* answered her prayer. Lauren's eyes watered, and she blinked to focus on the traffic ahead as she pulled back into the street. "Tell me all about them and all about your day."

"Well…" Zoey gave her a sly look. "One of them is a boy."

"Okay." This was new. Her daughter hadn't shown much interest in boys yet, maybe because some of them had been her worst tormentors.

"Yeah. I sat next to him in computer class, and we talked a lot. Then at lunch, when I was having trouble with my tray, he came over and took it." Her face glowed. "He took me over to a table with his sister. She's in my English class, and they're twins." She laughed. "But you wouldn't know it. He's real tall, like almost six feet. She's a little taller than me, maybe five-eight. He's got black hair, and she's a blonde. They both have blue eyes. They said they want me to sit with them at lunch every day."

Listening to her happy chatter, Lauren's heart filled with joy. "They sound very nice." More than that, maybe they would be her silent protectors if other students weren't so kind. She gave Zoey a quick, side-eyed glance. "Do they have names?"

Zoey snorted. "Duh. Of course, Mom. They're Bobby and Mandy Mattson, and they live on the Double Bar M Ranch. They want me to come out and ride horses with them."

While she continued to chatter on about her wonderful first day, Lauren could hardly keep her eyes on the road.

Why did her precious daughter's much-needed new friends have to be related to that horrible man who accused Lauren of stealing his valuable dog?

Chapter Two

"Everything looks great, Mom." Rob helped himself to a large portion of his favorite beef stew and grabbed two biscuits from the basket in front of his plate. The spicy aroma of the stew made his mouth water. "Nobody can cook like you, right, kids?"

"Right," the twins said in unison as they filled their plates.

"Can I have a peanut butter sandwich?" Eight-year-old Clementine frowned at the stew Mom had served her.

"Sorry, Clementine." Rob chuckled. "We're cattle ranchers. Gotta eat beef at least once a day."

She huffed out a dramatic sigh and wrinkled her nose as if the food on her plate smelled like something other than mouthwateringly delicious.

"Gramma, what are we gonna eat after you leave?" Bobby asked before shoveling a large spoonful into his mouth. Lady, who lay beside his chair, watched him but didn't beg for a bite.

"And who's going to teach my brother good manners when you're gone?" Mandy smirked at Bobby. "That was an awful big bite."

He returned a goofy glare and again shoveled a large spoonful into his mouth.

"I'm sure y'all can manage," Mom laughed. "Back in the day, cowboys learned to cook for themselves. As for their manners, well, everybody had better manners back then."

She set her fork down and sighed. "I'm starting to feel guilty about leaving you all."

"It's not too late to change your mind." Mandy's hopeful expression was mirrored on her brother's face.

"Yeah, Gramma." Clementine's voice was edged with a whine. "Not too late."

"Hey, now." Rob couldn't let their pleading get to Mom, no matter how much he wanted her to stay on the ranch where she'd lived for forty-five years since marrying Dad. "Your grandmother needs a break from taking care of you mavericks. Besides, Phoenix isn't that far. We'll have lots of visits."

"Yes, we will. Especially at Christmas." Mom picked up her fork. "Now, you three, how was your first day back to school?"

"It was fun." Clementine was always the first of his kids to speak up. "I saw all my friends, and I like my teacher."

"That's good, honey. It's real important to like your teacher." Rob eyed his older daughter. "Mandy?"

Her blue eyes twinkled. "We saw all our old friends, too, and we met a new girl and invited her out to ride this coming Saturday." She looked at Rob, raising her eyebrows as though she'd asked a question, not stated a plan.

"No problem. Just be sure you practice your own barrel racing. You need to keep that up so you'll be ready for the Miss Riverton Stampede next spring."

"Oh, Dad." Mandy rolled her eyes. "Been there, done that. Isn't it time to let somebody else wear the crown? I mean, I really enjoyed being Junior Miss Stampede, but I'd rather—"

"Aw, come on, sweetheart." Rob tried to keep his voice light, but she had no idea how much this meant to him. "It's a family tradition, and people expect the ladies in our family to compete. First Gramma, then your mom." He could finally speak about Jordyn without choking up. "See where it got them? As rodeo queens, they caught the attention of some pretty high-profile cowboys." He grinned playfully, but it was true. Mom had married Dad right after her reign as Miss Riverton Stampede ended, and Rob had put off proposing to Jordyn until her reign was almost over so she could keep her crown. "Right, Mom?"

"Don't put me in the middle of this." She held one hand up like a stop sign. "I loved being a rodeo queen and all the opportunities it gave me. But you have to let these kids find their own paths."

With that kind of support, maybe Rob would have an easier time influencing those paths once Mom moved out. No, that wasn't true. He might do all right raising Bobby, but Mandy and Clementine needed Mom's womanly influence. Still, he wouldn't fight her move.

"I want to be Miss Riverton Stampede." Clementine gave Rob a hopeful smile.

"Very good, sweetheart." He winked at her. "You just keep up with your riding lessons, and when you're old enough, you'll get your chance." He eyed Bobby. "Okay, enough about the women. How's it going with Lady today? You spend any time working her with the steers?"

"Yessir." He reached down and patted Lady's head. "I think she remembers some of her training, but she's not real enthusiastic about it. She mostly wants to hang out with me, not work the cattle with the other dogs."

He blew out a sigh. Just what he'd feared. That Parker woman and her daughter had ruined the best natural cow herding dog he'd ever had. "Well, keep at it." Maybe he'd have to work with Bobby and Lady himself.

He still hadn't decided whether or not to tell Will and Sam about his encounter with the Parkers. He didn't feel right letting his cousins continue to employ a dishonest woman in their law office. On the other hand, if they fired her, how would she support her daughter? Besides, Rob didn't have any actual evidence to prove Mrs. Parker stole Lady, except that the chip had been removed from Lady's shoulder. He should have gotten the name of that Santa Fe vet who treated the dog so he could check her story, but he wasn't about to ask her for it now.

"So, tell us more about your new friend," Mom said to the twins.

"Well, she's really sweet and really cute." Mandy shot a look at Bobby, but he didn't react. Good thing. It was way too early for his son to get interested in girls.

"Yeah, she's real nice and super-smart at computers." Bobby grinned. "A real computer geek, like me."

Geek? Rob hated that word but stifled the urge to scold his son. How could he raise the next owner of the Double Bar M when his heir apparent preferred computers to cattle?

"And what's her name?" Mom continued her interrogation.

"Zoey Parker." The twins spoke in unison, as they often did.

If a boulder had fallen on Rob's chest, he couldn't have felt more impact. The bite of beef he was about to swallow came near to choking him, but he managed to cough it out before it reached his throat. How could this be happening? How could his own children become traitors unaware?

"And her mother works for Will and Sam," Bobby said.

"Oh, how nice," Mom said. "Do they go to church?"

"I haven't seen them there." Bobby shrugged. "Hey, sis, we should invite Zoey to youth group."

"Sure thing."

As their conversation continued, Rob scrambled to sort out his tangled thoughts and feelings. He wanted nothing to do with Lauren Parker, but by befriending her daughter, his own children had shown what they were really made of. They weren't put off by her disability. In fact, hadn't even mentioned it. He couldn't be prouder of them for that omission. Now he just had to figure out how to help them keep their promise to take Zoey riding without having to encounter her mother. Fat chance of that. It was his responsibility to keep watch to be sure Zoey was safe as she rode, as he did with any guest to the ranch. Which meant, like it or not, he would be there when Zoey and her mother arrived on Saturday.

Lauren followed the directions on her phone's GPS, wishing for all she was worth that she and Zoey were going somewhere else, anywhere else, this Saturday. Why did she feel like she was headed for her execution, not for a fun and exciting opportunity for Zoey to learn something new, something that would help her develop her motor skills? Would they encounter Robert Mattson, or would his children be in charge of the horse riding?

Not that she had full confidence in two fifteen-year-olds being responsible enough to help Zoey learn to ride. But Lauren would stick close to catch Zoey if she started to fall.

"Look, Mom. There it is." Zoey had bounced with excitement in the passenger seat ever since they'd left their apartment. Now she pointed to the huge redbrick archway set some twenty yards off the highway. Emblazoned ironworks words across the arch announced Double Bar M Ranch.

"Yep." Lauren swallowed hard as she pulled up to the intercom on a post and punched the call button.

"Can I help you?" a youngish female voice said.

"It's me, Mandy," Zoey called out across the car.

"Zoeeeeey!"

Her squeal, followed by a buzzing sound and the whir of the well-oiled gate opening, didn't help Lauren's nerves. Somehow she managed to hide her emotions from Zoey as she negotiated the gravel driveway onto the property, past pastures and up to the beautiful wood frame house on the left. Like a white columned antebellum mansion, it stood on a hill above the Rio Grande. Several other houses and outbuildings dotted the vast property, including a huge red barn off to the right.

At the main house, complete with a white picket fence covered with late summer roses and sweet peas, a teen girl dashed out the door, followed by a tall, lanky teen boy and a little girl…and Lady.

"Park here," the girl called out as she waved a hand toward a spot beside the fence, then hurried over to Zoey's door.

Lauren got out and surveyed the property. With horseback riding their purpose for being here, she would have preferred to park closer to the barn so Zoey wouldn't have so far to walk. But she wouldn't embarrass her daughter by suggesting it.

Zoey was out of the car in a flash, falling to her knees to hug Lady, who wagged all over as she greeted her. "Oh, Daisy, I've missed you so much."

The other kids watched, their faces bright with innocent pleasure.

"Her name's Lady," the little girl said. "How do you know her?"

Zoey looked up at Lauren, her eyes filled with sadness. When Lauren realized they would be coming to this ranch, they'd talked about seeing Lady again, but that didn't mean Zoey would be able to hide how much she missed the dog. And now she could see how much the dog missed her.

"Hi, Mrs. Parker." The lanky boy, getting close to six feet tall, as Zoey had said, was definitely his father's son, at least in looks. "I'm Bobby."

"Hi, Bobby." Cute boy, and obviously much nicer than his namesake dad.

"I'm Mandy." The teen girl, close to five foot eight inches, also as Zoey had said, gently tugged on the younger one's blond ponytail. "This is Clementine."

"Aka Pest." The boy chucked the little one under the chin. "Or Short Stuff."

She grinned but kept her eyes on Zoey and repeated her question. "How do you know Lady?"

"These are the people who found Lady and took care of her," Mandy said. "Right, Mrs. Parker?"

"Right." So her father had told them, at least the older ones. "I'm glad to meet you. Thank you for inviting Zoey out to ride. She's never ridden—"

"They know, Mom." Zoey scolded her with a look.

All righty, then. This was Zoey's party, so Lauren would try her best to keep quiet.

"Let's go!" Mandy grasped Zoey's hand, not to help her but in a companionable way.

Lauren followed the kids and Lady across the barnyard toward the huge red structure, with Lady sticking close to Zoey. Would that cause a problem? Two other dogs trotted from the barn toward the group, tails wagging, and ate up the affection the kids gave them. A few cats dotted the area, but they appeared content to watch the action rather than take part. Maybe she should get Zoey a kitten, which would be so much easier to care for in their apartment.

"Mrs. Parker," Bobby said, "we're so grateful to you for taking care of Lady. I know you miss her, but we can give you a puppy, if you want one. That is, when she has one."

Zoey shot her a hopeful look.

"Thanks. We'll see." These purebred dogs were way out of her price range, and she doubted their father would just give one away.

As they entered the barn, Lauren fanned herself with her hand, waving away flies and animal odors but welcoming the shade after walking in the August sunshine. The kids didn't seem bothered by the heat or the smells. While they gave Zoey a tour of the huge building, Lauren hung back by the door.

She caught a glimpse of Robert Mattson and another man as they entered the building at the far end. Using broad gestures, he was apparently giving orders to the other man. Scurrying across the dirt floor in a less than dignified manner, she followed the kids into the second aisle. They stood outside a stall where a beautiful paint horse hung its head over the door and gave them an expectant look.

"This is Tripper. He's real gentle. A retired ol' cowpony, so he's our best ride for beginners." Bobby dug a carrot out of his back jeans pocket and handed it to Zoey. "You can give it to him."

Without missing a beat, Zoey did as he said. The horse lipped the carrot into its mouth and chewed, which involved some serious moisture.

"Ewww." Zoey giggled and wiped her hand on her jeans.

While the other kids laughed, Lauren failed to hide her grimace. Good thing none of them looked her way. Lady moved closer to Zoey, gazing up at her as if making sure she was all right.

"You can't be finicky around horses," Mandy said. "If it's not slobber, it's manure."

"And before you ride—" Robert Mattson appeared around the corner of the aisle "—you muck out the stall. Work before pleasure."

Despite the heat, Lauren felt a chill sweep down her back.

"Hey, Dad." The twins spoke together, and little Clementine hurried over to hug her father. He patted her on the head.

"Hey." He gave Lauren a brief glance, clear annoyance on his face.

A wave of anxiety swept into her chest. Oh, how she did *not* want to be here. "Hi."

He walked over to Zoey, and his expression turned hospitable. "Welcome to the Double Bar M Ranch, Zoey. You ready for some barn chores before you ride?"

"Yessir." From her big grin, Zoey seemed not to remember that their previous encounter had been less than pleasant. "Gimme that shovel, and I'll get to work."

He chuckled, turning his face from stern to undeniably

handsome. Lauren had to look away. Her ex had been charming and handsome. Especially when he acted like Mr. Nice
Guy around people he wanted to impress.

Mandy put a bridle on Tripper, led him out of the stall
and handed the lead to Clementine, who tugged him several
yards down the aisle. At Mandy's direction, Zoey picked up
the shovel, struggling a bit with its weight.

"I'll do it." Bobby reached for the shovel.

"No. I got this." Shrugging away from him, Zoey worked
hard to scoop up some of the soiled straw. After three tries, she
succeeded, then dumped it in the nearby wheelbarrow. Only a
little spilled off onto the floor. Lady followed her every move,
almost like she wanted to help.

"Great job." Mandy grabbed another shovel and joined her.

Robert stepped over to Lauren and tilted his hat back from
his forehead. "Is she gonna be all right?"

His whispered words sent an odd little shudder down her
side. She looked up into his blue eyes, and his tall, broad-
shouldered, very masculine presence tickled her feminine
heart. *Oh, my. I'm my own worst enemy.* She looked down
and stepped away from him.

"Yes. She's fine." Did she sound as snippy to him as she
did to herself?

From his annoyed expression, the answer was yes. But what
did he expect? He hadn't apologized for accusing her of stealing Lady. Hadn't really thanked her for rescuing that sweet
little dog that clearly favored Zoey today.

"By the way, I have Lady's shot record in my car. I'll leave
it with you." She spared him a glance. "You can call the vet
and ask about the chip. Or the lack of chip."

He didn't speak for a moment. Finally, he leaned back
against the wall and crossed his arms. "I'll do that."

How rude. If Zoey's happiness and much-needed exercise

were not at stake, she'd take her daughter home right now and never come back.

After they spread fresh straw over the floor of the stall, Mandy and Zoey handed the shovels to Bobby to put away.

"Ready to saddle up?" Mandy asked Zoey.

"More than ready."

Watching her daughter struggle through the saddling procedure, Lauren had to clench her fists to keep from helping her. A glance at Robert revealed he seemed to have the same problem. At last the job was done.

"Here you go." Bobby half squatted and offered cupped hands to lift Zoey into the saddle.

"Here I go." She cast a nervous grin in Lauren's direction. Lauren returned a thumbs-up.

"Oops. Almost forgot your safety helmet." Bobby straightened and grabbed a black riding helmet from a nearby hook and handed it to Zoey.

"Oh, yeah." She laughed as she put it on and managed to snap the strap without too much trouble. "Gotta protect this crazy head of mine."

The kids also laughed, and Lauren smiled. Her daughter's sense of humor had smoothed over many awkward situations in her young life. She'd stopped wearing her own everyday safety helmet just last year, but today she was willing to wear this one.

Across the aisle, Lauren saw a sign. "Notice: This is an equine facility. All activities on these grounds are subject to the Equine Inherent Risk Law." She would have to check that law when she went to work on Monday. She'd learned a great deal about New Mexico law over the past few months, necessary information for her job. But none were as personally important to her as this one.

Arms still folded across his broad chest, Robert watched the kids like a hawk. Was he proud of their care and skilled instructions to Zoey, or was he sticking close hoping to avoid a lawsuit?

With Mandy on Tripper's opposite side and Bobby lifting, Zoey was soon in the saddle with her sneakers settled in the stirrups. She grinned broadly as Mandy showed her how to hold the reins.

"Okay, let's head out to the corral." Mandy grasped Tripper's bridle and walked toward a broad doorway at the side of the barn.

Lauren followed, and little Clementine skipped along beside her dad, who was focused on the others. Lady trotted close to Tripper, careful to avoid his hooves.

The riding lesson went on longer than Lauren expected. Mandy led Tripper around the corral with great patience, while Bobby and even Robert watched with sustained interest. Zoey was having the time of her life.

"She's a natural." Robert's observation startled Lauren.

"You don't have to say that." Sometimes people tried to be helpful by giving Zoey more praise than was warranted.

"I call 'em as I see 'em." Robert snorted. "You need to have more faith in your daughter."

Lauren swallowed a sharp retort. She refused to argue with this man. Besides, she had plenty of faith in Zoey's can-do attitude. She preferred honest assessment rather than phony praise.

The morning wore on, but the kids were having so much fun, no one seemed in a hurry for the riding lesson to end. Worse still, Lauren had hoped one time on horseback would be enough, but the kids were already making plans for next Saturday.

"Hey, Mrs. Parker." Mandy held up her phone. "My gramma just sent me a text saying she'd like you and Zoey to stay for lunch."

She started to make an excuse, but heard a quiet groan from

the big man beside her. How rude, especially since she had no intention of staying on the ranch any longer than necessary.

"You can't say no," Bobby said. "Gramma makes the best tuna salad in the world." He spoke as if it were a done deal.

Lauren scrambled for an honest excuse, but the hopeful look on Zoey's face made it impossible.

"Please, Mom."

She released a long sigh. "That's very kind. Please text back that we accept."

Robert groaned again, and Lauren could almost feel disapproval radiating from him. Which made his large presence almost feel menacing.

"On second thought—"

"No." His voice had a harsh edge. "When my mother invites you, you come. Got that?"

Lauren was too stunned to respond. There was something in his voice that went beyond giving orders. She should pack up Zoey and leave now, but curiosity made her want to meet the woman who commanded such obedience from her forty-something son.

Chapter Three

Rob felt trapped. Mom hadn't invited anybody to a meal since Dad died two years ago, and her two closest friends had already moved to Phoenix. He wasn't about to deny her the pleasure of having guests, even if those guests included Lauren Parker. So he'd bite the bullet and tolerate her for Mom's sake.

Zoey was another matter. He was glad to have her stay. She was the most uncomplicated teenager he'd ever met, very different from some of the twins' other friends, who clearly hung around them because their last name was Mattson. He'd known that kind of hanger-on in his own high school years, so they were easy to spot. Zoey didn't seem to have an agenda other than to enjoy the twins' company. Even Clementine got some of her attention. How could such a sweet girl be the daughter of a dog thief? It did bother him that Lady seemed glued to Zoey's side, but enough time with Bobby should fix that.

"How can I help you?" Lauren stood at Mom's elbow while Mom sliced tomatoes on the kitchen counter.

"Thanks. You can set the table." His mom nodded toward the round kitchen table. "Plates and glasses in that cupboard." She pointed with her chin. "Fill the glasses with ice from the fridge door. Is sweet tea okay?"

Rob watched from the doorway as Lauren followed Mom's instructions. The two women chatted like women do, seeming to hit it off right away. Great. Just what Rob needed. His mother being friends with his enemy. Maybe Mom would move to Phoenix before he could prove Lauren's dishonesty. She was waiting for the completion of her condo, so her move-in date was uncertain. Maybe by Christmas. No, that was no reason to want Mom gone. Without her help, he had no idea what he'd do with Clementine while he took care of the ranch and his responsibilities to the Cattlemen's Association and the Riverton Stampede Committee.

The kids kept the conversation around the table going as they rehashed the morning's ride to Mom. She listened intently, while Mrs. Parker seemed more interested in her plate. More important, Lady had settled beside Zoey's chair rather than Bobby's. How was Rob going to break that attachment when border collies were known for their loyalty?

Clementine stared across the table at Zoey. "Why do you talk so funny?"

Rob sucked in a breath. "Clementine, that's rude!"

She winced at his harsh tone, but he couldn't let her thoughtlessness go uncorrected. Mom looked surprised and disappointed, as did the twins. Mrs. Parker appeared unfazed. Maybe other kids had asked her daughter the same question.

"It's okay, Mr. Mattson." Zoey smiled like she'd just received a compliment. "It's natural for kids to wonder about my goofy ways. It's like this, Clem." Zoey had already adopted the nickname Rob hated, probably because it was short and easier for her to pronounce. "Sometimes something goes wonky when a baby is born that makes them have cerebral palsy." She grimaced. Or maybe it was one of her uncontrolled facial movements. As usual, a little hum preceded her words. "When my mom saw I wasn't doing stuff babies are supposed to do—" she gave Mrs. Parker a sweet smile "—she made me exercise, so I can do lots more than I would have if I'd just stayed in bed all the time. Like, I wore braces on my legs so I could learn to walk, but I don't have to wear them anymore."

"One thing's sure," Bobby piped up. "It sure didn't affect your brain." Seated next to Clementine, he tweaked his little sister's nose. "She's the smartest one in our computer class." He faced Zoey. "Which reminds me, can you stay after lunch and help me with my programming assignment?"

"No way," Mandy said. "She's going to help me with my English essay—"

"Whoa. Put the brakes on." Mrs. Parker laughed—an undeniably pleasant sound—and her face took on the same maternal glow Rob had noticed before, which made her pretty face even prettier. Unlike his relationship with his own teens, these two communicated well. How could he think of putting Mrs. Parker in jail when her daughter so obviously needed her? Would Zoey's father step up to take care of her?

"Sorry to spoil your homework fun," Mrs. Parker continued. "But we have some errands to run, then Zoey needs to rest after her busy morning. And, of course, we have laundry." She gave Mom a look women often shared.

"Oh, yes." Mom laughed.

The twins sighed in unison, but nodded their understanding as well.

"Lauren," Mom said, "will you and Zoey come to church with us tomorrow? We attend Riverton Community Church."

"Zoey has to come to youth group with us tomorrow night," Mandy added.

"Whoa." Why had Rob echoed Lauren's word? "I'm sure Mrs. Parker and Zoey have their own church to attend."

"Please call me Lauren." She turned those gorgeous eyes toward him, but without the flirtatious eyelash batting some women sent his way.

Fine with him, but he wasn't about to form an attachment with this woman. "Sure. Call me Rob."

"Or you can call him Big Boss." Bobby smirked, earning

himself a swat on the shoulder from Rob. "Hey, I'm just telling it like it is. After all, that's what our cowhands call him."

"And you may call me Andrea," Mom said. "Now that we know who everybody is, what about church?"

"Well…" Lauren eyed Zoey, whose hopeful smile let her opinion be known. "How about we meet you there?"

That settled, they finished lunch, then started in on Mom's peach cobbler made with her recently home-canned New Mexico peaches and covered with fresh cream from one of their two milk cows.

"This is delicious, Andrea," Lauren said. "And Bobby sure was right about your tuna salad. It's the best I've ever eaten. Will you share your recipe?"

"Thank you." Mom beamed. "Of course you may have my recipe."

They chatted about Mom's "secret sauce," which generated more of that female bonding Rob didn't like to see between these two. If that wasn't enough, as their guests were leaving, Lady tried to climb into Lauren's little Honda with Zoey and whined when Bobby pulled her back.

"No, Lady." Bobby held on to her new collar. "You have to stay with me." He didn't seem as bothered by Lady's new attachment as Rob had hoped.

Zoey seemed to struggle with tears. Then she sniffed and put on a bright smile. "Thanks for a great morning."

Lauren glanced at Rob with a guarded expression. What was her problem? "Yes, thank you for a lovely morning."

"Next time *you* have to ride, Mrs. Parker." Mandy offered her a challenging grin.

"Ha. That'll be the day." Now Lauren smiled. "See you tomorrow at church." She ducked her head and climbed into her little car, started it, then lowered the window and held out some papers to Rob. "Here's Lady's shot record and the business card for that vet in Santa Fe. You be sure to call him, okay?"

Rob stared at the card, which looked like it had been run over by a truck. Where had she found it? On the roadside? Maybe that was how she'd concocted the story about the vet. As for the shot record, it could easily have been printed out from any computer.

He watched as they drove away, telling himself he just wanted to be sure the new sensor worked and would open the front gate as her car approached. Who was he kidding? She was a beautiful woman with a lovely daughter who, despite his suspicions *and* determination not to like her, was starting to get under his skin. Good thing they were going to church tomorrow. Maybe Pastor Tim's sermon would convict her, and she would admit she had something to do with Lady's dognapping. Yeah. That was it. She just needed to admit she'd done wrong, and they could go from there.

Every time Lauren took Zoey into a new experience, she worried about how people would treat her daughter, which was probably why she'd put off going to church here in Riverton. But from the moment they'd stepped out of the car, they'd been greeted by friendly folks of every age. Several teens waved and called out to Zoey, and she responded in kind. Mandy and Bobby, followed by cute little Clementine, ran across the church's front lawn, greeting them as though they hadn't seen each other in weeks instead of spending the previous morning together.

"You missed Sunday school." Mandy looped her arm around Zoey's and led the way toward the redbrick structure. "You have to come earlier next week. Let's sit together for the main service."

Lauren had no choice but to follow, even when Rob joined them. Andrea followed Zoey's example and looped her arm around Lauren's as though they were old friends instead of new acquaintances. How could such a lovely woman be the mother of a bully like Robert Mattson?

The music was a blend of praise songs and old standards, both of which lifted Lauren's heart in worship. The minister, Pastor Tim, gave an inspiring message from II Timothy about following one's holy calling, reminding her to get serious about her own personal Bible study. After the service, Andrea invited them to lunch at a local restaurant, but Lauren declined.

"Zoey's looking forward to youth group this evening, but she'll need to rest this afternoon."

"Another time, then," Andrea said.

Robert sauntered over to them. "What did you think of the sermon?"

This was the first time he'd shown interest in her opinion, and for some silly reason, her heart skipped a beat. "It was very nice. I like the pastor's down-to-earth style and his preaching from God's Word."

"Huh." His soft grunt almost sounded like he didn't believe her. He stared at her for a moment, and she had a ridiculous urge to squirm under his scrutiny. All pleasant feelings disappeared, and she looked away.

"Hey, folks." Will Mattson and his new bride, Olivia, joined them. He greeted Robert with a handshake. "Lauren, I'm glad to see you here."

After all around greetings, Will nudged Robert with his fist. "So, I see you've finally met our very accomplished paralegal."

The teasing look in his blue eyes hinted at matchmaking. Obviously her boss was not reading the room correctly. No way would she ever be interested in a bully like Robert Mattson. In fact, she had no interest in any kind of romance. Her daughter and her job took all of her time and energy, so why complicate their lives by adding a man? But even as she settled on that thought, a wave of sadness followed. She was doing the best she could as a mother, but she would always regret that Zoey would never know a father's love and nurturing. Once Zoey had been diagnosed with cerebral palsy, Singleton walked out and never set eyes on her again. As for Zoey, she'd only seen him on television, never knowing he was her father. And Lauren was happy to keep it that way as long as she could.

That evening, when they arrived at the church, the gym was alive with activity. Teens had already started playing volleyball, and as they had that morning, they greeted Zoey and invited her to play. Without asking Lauren, she joined Mandy on the court.

Lauren considered stopping her. If someone spiked the ball and it hit Zoey in the head, it could cause serious injury. Even a light hit might cause a seizure like the ones Zoey occasionally experienced. Should she have brought her daughter's helmet? No, unlike yesterday when she was riding Tripper, Zoey would never wear it when she was among her peers.

Lord, please protect her.

Lauren sat on the lowest bench in the bleachers and watched as her daughter stood near the net and kept an eye on the fast-moving ball.

"Mind if I sit here?" The ever-present Robert Mattson parked his large person a few feet away from her.

Really? You're going to sit by me? Glancing at him, she managed a half smile before turning her eyes back to Zoey. "Sure."

"Looks like the kids are having fun." Robert waved a hand toward the court.

She managed a noncommittal "Uh-huh."

"If I know my son, he's keeping an eye on the refreshment table."

Across the gym, a long table had been set up with sodas, bottled water, ice cream, cookies and chips. Should she have brought something to add to the snacks? Too late now.

Recorded praise music wafted through the air and blended with the shouts and laughter of the teens, echoing off the gym walls. Parents watching the informal game chatted in the bleachers behind her.

The volleyball popped over the net toward Zoey, and she managed to lift her hands in time to send it flying toward one of her teammates. As they cheered her good move, Lauren swallowed the lump in her throat.

"She's doing real well." Rob's unexpected praise startled Lauren.

"Yes." Lauren glanced his way again. "Your kids, too."

"Yeah. They're pretty good at most sports."

Why was he being so chatty? Okay, she could do chatty with him. What father didn't like to brag about his kids? With this being the school's fall semester, only one thing came to her mind.

"Does Bobby play football?"

He snorted softly. "More or less. He's not crazy about it, but he manages to keep up the family tradition."

"Let me guess. You were the starting quarterback." She punctuated her cheeky question with a laugh.

He grinned. Actually *grinned*, revealing a dimple on his left cheek she hadn't noticed before. "Guilty. But as a senior, not a sophomore. He's got two years to work up to it."

Poor kid. What did Bobby want to do? "And I suppose it's a birthright for him?"

"Birthright?" Rob shook his head. "Huh. Never thought of it that way." He swiped a hand down his cheek, where a five-o'clock shadow added to his overall handsome cowboy appearance. "It's just what my family always does."

That explained a lot. "And if he prefers to do something else?"

"Huh." His favorite word. "He still has time to get his head on right."

"Zoey says he's into computer programming. What's not right about that?"

He gave her a long look. "He's gonna take over the Double Bar M Ranch one day. I can see computers for the business side of things, but ranching's a hands-on enterprise that takes time and dedication and hard physical work."

"Hmm." Lauren turned her attention back to the game. Just as she'd suspected from their few encounters, this man ruled his family rather than guided them. That was no way to raise kids.

Zoey was doing her best as the ball came her way another time, but Lauren could see she was struggling to keep her arms up. Which meant she was getting tired. Time to pull her out of the game. Before she could act, the ball sailed over the net and banged Zoey in the forehead, knocking her down, her head hitting the wooden floor with an audible thump.

The noisy gym fell silent. The youth pastor and other adults rushed to Zoey.

And Lauren's world stopped.

Chapter Four

Instinct and experience shook Lauren from the iron grip of panic. She rushed to her daughter. To her relief, Zoey was conscious and blinking her eyes, a tiny grin—or grimace?—forming on her lips as she tried to sit up.

"Lie still, honey." Lauren brushed Zoey's hair back from her forehead, where a red mark was still spreading.

"Oops." Zoey spoke softly. "I missed the ball."

"Yeah, but the ball sure didn't miss you," some boy nearby quipped.

Nervous laughter erupted until a female voice hissed, "Shh."

The same woman knelt beside Lauren. "Ma'am, I'm a nurse. Will you let me check her out?" Without waiting for an answer, she nudged Lauren aside and checked Zoey's eyes and neck.

"Please be careful," Lauren whispered. "She has CP."

Zoey scolded her with a frown. She hated it when Lauren announced her condition.

"I see." The nurse took Zoey's pulse. "Then we'll wait for the paramedics to bring a collar and take her to the hospital for tests."

"Okay, kids." The youth pastor spoke in a cheerful but authoritative tone. "Let's break for snacks while the grown-ups handle this." He herded the twenty or so youths toward the refreshment table.

"Does this mean I won't get any ice cream?" Zoey added

a comical whine to her question. As always, she was making light of a worrisome situation. Sometimes it made it hard for Lauren to know how serious her injuries were.

"Don't worry, kiddo." Robert Mattson's words, spoken right behind Lauren, sent an odd feeling down her back. Had he been this close all along? "We'll make sure to save you some. What's your favorite flavor?"

"Strawberry." Zoey sent him a wobbly smile. "Thanks."

While the other adults managed the youth and children, eventually sending them to their evening classes, Robert stayed nearby, though Lauren couldn't imagine why. Despite his twins' objections, he'd sent them with the others.

Minutes later, paramedics arrived and secured Zoey's neck with a collar before lifting her onto the lowered gurney and raising it to transport height.

"I'll go with you," Robert said.

"Thanks, but that's not necessary." Lauren nodded toward Becca, the nurse. "She's going."

"Yeah, Rob." Becca waved him away. "You just take care of my kids for me. We women can manage this."

"I said I'm going." Robert retrieved his Stetson from the bleachers and plopped it on his head. "And you, Becca, can take care of *my* kids."

"Let's go." The lead paramedic pushed the gurney toward the door. "ER's waiting."

Becca gave Lauren an apologetic shrug. "I'll be praying for you."

Lauren had no choice but to follow the paramedics to the ambulance and climb in beside Zoey. A second before the attendant closed the door, she saw Robert get into his monster black pickup. She didn't want this bossy bully to accompany her, but right now she had to take care of her daughter.

In the back of her mind, she could only wonder what went on in this community that required everybody to do exactly what Robert Mattson said. It almost seemed like he said "jump" and they asked "how high?"

After church this morning, Rob had decided the best way to uncover Lauren's dishonesty was to stick close to her whenever possible. So he'd sought her out and sat beside her in the bleachers, hoping casual conversation would uncover her true character. But all her focus had been on Zoey, as with any good mother. He'd been as upset as everyone else when the sweet little gal had been slammed to the floor by that volleyball. If either of his daughters had CP, he wouldn't let her go near a volleyball court or any other sport. Not after what happened to his sister and his wife. But try telling a modern woman what she couldn't do, and a man got in plenty of trouble, as he'd learned the hard way.

But he wasn't about to let Zoey miss out on any treatment at the hospital. Had Lauren's health insurance from Will's law office kicked in yet? If not, he'd pay for Zoey's treatments, no matter how much Lauren objected. After all, his kids had invited Zoey to church and encouraged her to play, so he was responsible for her welfare at church as much as at the ranch.

He pulled into the hospital parking lot right after the ambulance and followed Lauren inside through the ER entrance. In spite of the blast of hospital smells striking him—rubbing alcohol, sickness, cleaning solution—all of which reminded him of both Jordyn's and Dad's deaths, he was proud of this little hospital. His family had been its major donors over the years so citizens of Riverton didn't have to drive to Santa Fe or Albuquerque for special tests and treatments. When Dad died, he'd left a large bequest to purchase an MRI scanner and other vital equipment in an area where cowboys sometimes suffered serious injuries in their daily work. Rob knew Dad had done it because of Jordyn's death. If they'd had that MRI scanner when she had her accident, the doctors might have been able to save her, but the X-ray that had revealed her broken neck missed the fatal damage to her brain.

He shoved away the bitter memory, which could still make his belly ache after four years. Time to focus on the young girl being checked by the new ER resident.

"Mom, you'll need to take out her earrings." The doctor handed Lauren a medical form on a clipboard. "While we get that MRI done, I need you to fill out her medical history."

"Yes, of course." Lauren brushed a hand over Zoey's cheek, then carefully removed the jewelry from her earlobes. "You okay, honey?"

"Yeah. I'm fine." Zoey seemed more annoyed than injured.

"Not worried about going into that MRI tube?"

"Been there, done that, Mom."

Brave kid. Rob grinned at her over Lauren's shoulder, and Zoey returned a sweet smile as the orderly wheeled her from the ER cubicle. Lauren looked his way and scowled. Or maybe just frowned.

"You really don't need to stay. I've got this."

That was what Jordyn had always said. Except she hadn't always "got this."

"Not a problem. You'll need a ride back to the church to pick up your car after she's done here."

Sighing, Lauren shook her head. "Whatever." She wandered from the ER to the nearest waiting room, plunked herself down on the gray Naugahyde couch and filled out the form. That finished, she stared up at the mounted TV where a '70s comedy show was playing without sound.

"You want to hear it? It'll make the time pass faster." He reached up toward the controls on the side, but she'd already picked up the remote and clicked off the show. "Guess that answers that."

She grabbed a gossip magazine from the coffee table, wrinkled her nose and set it back down.

Rob chuckled. "Not the best reading material. But they do have a library. Can I get you a book?"

She stared up at him for several seconds. "Don't you have something more important to do than, for lack of a better word, *entertain* me?"

He chuckled again. Not many people in these parts talked to him that way. Against everything that made sense, he liked her spunk. But then, that kind of brashness could be a defense to hide her deceitfulness. Jordyn had always used bossiness as a smoke screen when she went behind his back on matters they disagreed on, especially when it came to the kids. Again, he smothered the unpleasant memory.

"I'll get us some coffee." He walked away, hoping the coffee machine wasn't as bad as he'd heard. Sad to say, it was. But he brought her a cup anyway and set it on the table beside her, then sipped from his own cup.

"Thanks." She took a careful sip of the steaming brew and made a grimace too cute to describe. "You trying to poison me?" She shuddered and set the cup back down.

"This is gourmet stuff." He made a show of drinking more of his own and managed not to choke on it. "You should taste the coffee we have on our cattle drives. Nothing like a little trail dust to flavor your morning joe."

"Cattle drives?" She picked up the cup and drank another sip. It seemed to go down easier this time. "You still drive cattle?" She blinked those gray-green eyes, and a dangerous little tickle threaded through his chest. "Like in the Old West?"

Who didn't know that? Oh, yeah. City women from back East.

"Sure do. Every spring we haul the cattle up into the Sangre de Cristo Mountains in semis as far as the trucks can go. From there, we mount up and drive them farther up to the best summer pasture."

"Wow. All of that so we can eat steak and hamburgers." Her interest seemed genuine.

"Yes, ma'am." He was warming to his favorite topic, and it helped to have an interested audience. Or was she just faking it? Since Jordyn died, lots of women had shown interest in whatever he said, but their real interest was in his wealth and position in the community. He'd have to be on guard with this one. Her natural feminine attractiveness might charm some men, so he'd have to fortify his own defenses.

"Our roundup's in a couple of weeks. I'm hoping Bobby will have Lady trained back into her instinctive herding by then."

A shadow crossed her face, and she looked away. "I hope so, too."

He sat across from her and considered her words. Did she really hope Lady would remember her early training and be worth the investment he'd made in her? The two pups she'd had while she was missing were healthy and strong, but their dad was a mongrel. Rob had let Will and Olivia keep the little mutts for their newly blended family. If nothing else, Lady could still be a good breeding dog. Or not. A mother dog was always an important part of the training, and if she didn't teach her pedigreed pups how to herd, his whole purpose for buying her would be wasted.

"Mrs. Parker?" The doctor entered the waiting room carrying a CD case. "She came through just fine. We'll have the results within twenty-four hours after our radiologist reads the scan, but you can have this for your own records."

"Thanks." Lauren accepted the disk and handed him the clipboard. "Is she ready to go?"

"Yes, ma'am." He read the medical form as he stepped toward the hallway, with Lauren and Rob following. "Hmm. Considering her CP and these seizures she had this summer, you need to keep her activities to a minimum this week to be sure she doesn't have a setback. Just to be safe, I'm writing you a script for Keppra, which she needs to take every day, and one for pain in case she needs it. Make sure she stays hydrated, and keep her at home. Maybe get her teachers to email her schoolwork."

"Oh." Lauren stopped. "You mean she can't go to school?"

Rob didn't wait for Doc to answer. He whipped out his phone and called Will. "Hey, Cuz, you don't mind Lauren bringing Zoey to work this week." He quickly explained the situation. "Great. I'll send over a cot." He ended the call. "There. All set up." To his shock, Lauren stood gaping at him, anger emanating from her entire body.

"Who, just *who* do you think you are?" Hands fisted at her slender waist, she sputtered out the words. "I'm perfectly capable of taking care of my daughter."

Whoa. He hadn't expected this reaction. Most people were glad for help. What was it with this woman?

Lauren couldn't remember when she'd been this angry. Not even when Singleton announced his rejection of Zoey and his plans to divorce her. Not even when her ex had filed a petition to lower her child support payments. Worst of all, Robert Mattson stood there looking shocked at her outburst when he'd just taken over her life. To her further annoyance, the doctor seemed just as shocked. Oh, right. How could she forget? Everybody treated this wealthy rancher with the utmost respect.

"Take me to my daughter." Lauren looked down the hallway.

"Uh…" The young man had the nerve to look at Robert as if checking to see if he should do as she said. Lauren didn't spare the rancher a glance, but he must have given the okay, because the doc said, "Yes, ma'am. This way."

In the recovery cubicle outside the MRI room, Zoey rested against the partially raised pillows of her bed, her arms crossed in annoyance. "Are we done yet?" She looked past Lauren and smiled. "Did you save me some strawberry ice cream?"

Again, Lauren didn't have to turn around to know Robert was on her heels.

"Sure did. Well, I told Mandy to."

"Thanks." Zoey's sweet smile should have encouraged Lauren, but aimed at Robert, it made her heart sink. Her daughter was getting attached to this man.

"You ready to go, young lady?" a nurse asked as she pushed a wheelchair into the cubicle.

"I can walk."

"Sorry, miss. Hospital policy." The doctor spoke up before Lauren could object. Why was he sticking around? Oh, yeah. Probably to impress Robert Mattson. "Now, you do what your mom says, okay? Keep your activities to a minimum. Take your meds. No school for a week. Then I want to see you in my office on Friday. And no more volleyball, at least for a while. Got it?"

"Got it." Sighing, Zoey teared up.

Lauren felt her own tears coming, but she refused to let them form. "Okay, then. Let's go."

She barely managed to deflect Robert's help as she and the nurse helped Zoey from the bed and into the wheelchair. She had no choice but to accept his ride back to the church and her own vehicle, but that would be the end of it. Somehow she would break free from his hovering presence, or else she feared she would fall into the Mattson trap everyone else seemed caught in.

As he'd told Will, Robert delivered a cot to the law office early Monday morning. Will and Sam had opted for partitioning the current location, and the contractor had already framed in several walls. The cot fit nicely behind Lauren's desk in the reception area and would allow Zoey to nap when needed.

"We'll miss you at school," Mandy said. She, Bobby and

Clementine had come with their father, bringing a surprise that didn't appear to please him—Lady. The darling dog greeted Zoey with eager but gentle kisses and furious tail wagging, then nestled beside her on the cot and gazed up into her face with obvious affection.

"We thought maybe you could keep Lady company," Bobby said. "She gets lonely out on the ranch when we're in school." What a sweet boy to make it sound like Zoey was doing them a favor. He must have learned that kindness from his grand-mother.

While Zoey exclaimed with delight, Lauren heard Robert's grunt of disapproval but ignored it. Actually, she found his reaction to his kids' generosity oddly amusing. So, not every-body jumped through Robert Mattson's hoops.

No, that wasn't a good reaction. No matter what everybody else did or didn't do, his kids should respect and obey their parent, just as she'd taught Zoey to do. As for her, she had no idea how to stop Robert's interference in her and Zoey's lives when nearly everybody else bent over backward to please him.

Chapter Five

❧

When Lady jumped up on the cot, settled beside Zoey and stared up into her face, Rob knew he'd made a mistake to give in to Bobby. Why was his son so willing to encourage his dog to bond with somebody else? Or re-bond. Lady had already attached to the girl over the summer, and this would only solidify her loyalty and affection.

Rob wouldn't give up though. In less than two weeks when he took Bobby on his first cattle drive, Lady would go, too. A week of being with the herd and learning from the other dogs should restore her training as a pup, when she'd taken to the job like a natural.

"Thank you so much for bringing her." Zoey's bright smile and good color seemed to indicate she was recovering from her accident last evening.

"Thank you for the cot." Lauren didn't look his way as she spoke.

"Mornin', boys." Rob nodded to his cousins, who had come out to the reception area. At twelve and thirteen years younger than Rob, they were used to this old-fashioned cowboy name for them.

"Mornin'," Will said. "I see you and Lauren finally met." He arched one eyebrow and gave Rob a crooked grin. "I mean other than church yesterday."

Rob ignored the comment and the insinuation that went

with it. His newlywed cousin had been trying to fix him up with this woman ever since his wedding, but Rob had managed to dodge the introduction. Time to change the subject.

"I like what you're doing here." He waved a hand toward the framed-in walls. "But if it doesn't work out, you can still use my Fourth Street building."

"Thanks," Sam said. "We'll keep that in mind."

"Hey there, Lady." Will bent down and ruffled the fur behind the dog's ears. "We still need to get you out to my place to say hello to your pups."

"Think she'll remember them?" Clementine petted Lady.

"Or they'll remember her?" Mandy added.

Rob didn't want this to go any further. "Time to get you kids to school. We'll pick Lady up this afternoon. Ma'am." He nodded to Lauren, then herded the kids out to the truck. She'd barely said a word, just mumbled "thank you" when he brought in the cot. No surprise there. She'd been real quiet last evening as they drove back to the church. Was it stubbornness? Pride? Or, to be fair, just a mother worried about her daughter?

He let the twins off at the high school, then Clementine at the elementary school. Before she climbed out, his youngest paused with one foot out of the back door.

"I think Lady likes Zoey. I think we should let her keep her." Before he could explain why that wasn't going to happen, she jumped to the concrete sidewalk, slammed the back door and ran to greet her friends.

No, Lady wasn't going to stay with Zoey, no matter how much they'd bonded. He'd make sure she found her way back to herding, even if he had to take over the training himself.

Despite working full-time, Lauren had kept an eye on Zoey all summer through several daily FaceTime chats. At fifteen, her daughter could stay home alone, and it had helped to have

Daisy...*Lady* with her at all times, as well as a helpful neighbor lady who checked on her. But now that she required constant observation in case her fall on the gym floor brought on a seizure, having her here in the office gave Lauren great peace of mind. Even though she'd been offended by Robert's high-handedness in calling Will about the situation *and* deciding to bring the cot rather than asking if she wanted it, she had to admit it was a good plan. Somehow she'd find a way to do more than mumble a weak "thank you" to him. Bake cookies? No. Last Saturday at the ranch, she'd noticed his lovely mother kept the Mattson cookie jar full.

Nothing in Lauren's power or ability could even the score with the wealthy rancher so she wouldn't owe him anything. She'd had a hard enough time at the hospital making sure the clerk in the billing department accepted Zoey's Medicaid rather than Robert's credit card, and she refused his offer to pay for the Keppra prescription and pain medication at the overnight pharmacy. Why did he keep trying to take over her life? Somehow she had to regain control.

For now, she needed to concentrate on the adoption and foster parent petitions on her desk. As she'd told Robert, it was unprofessional to mix personal matters with work. And yet, here she was, bringing her daughter to work, thanks to him.

The prescription from the ER doctor didn't entirely erase Zoey's headache, and the anticonvulsant medication made her vision a little blurry, but she still managed to use her laptop to connect with her teachers through the high school's website. Since the pandemic, the faculty had continued to post their lessons online so students could keep up with their classes. Zoey was good with computers, thanks to her uncle, Lauren's older brother, a software engineer. Most of her family had blamed Lauren for the divorce due to Singleton's charming ways and a few outright lies, but her brother, David, had stood by her.

"Can I bring you ladies some lunch from the diner?" Will

stood by the front door putting on his Stetson. Backlit against the daylight, he looked like a younger version of Robert.

"Yes!" Zoey sat up a little too fast, and her eyelids flickered. Lady went on alert, sitting up to focus on Zoey's face even before Lauren could register alarm. Zoey's expression settled as she added, "Cheeseburger with fries."

Will laughed. "You sound like my neph—my son." He still stumbled over calling the nephew he recently adopted *son.* "He always wants burger and fries. Lauren, how about you?"

"Burger and fries sounds good." Lauren reached for her purse.

Will put up his hand. "I've got this. You ladies have been working hard this morning." He'd given Zoey some envelopes to stuff, a job she'd managed better than Lauren expected. "I'll be back in a jiff."

Before he could go out the door, Robert burst in, his arms full of take-out bags. Lady jumped off the cot and wandered over to greet him.

"Zoey, I brought you some lunch and that long overdue strawberry ice cream. I noticed you didn't feel like eating the ice cream Mandy saved for you last night, so I hope this makes up for it."

He set a soft drink—in a moist plastic cup—on Lauren's desk, barely missing some important papers. She managed to snatch them up just in time.

"Hey, watch it." She couldn't keep the annoyance from her voice.

"Yeah, watch it." Will's tone was more teasing than cross.

"Right." Robert handed a bag to Will. "Put this in your fridge. It's Zoey's ice cream."

"Sure thing." Like everybody else, Will did what Robert said.

"Thanks, Mr. Mattson," Zoey said.

"You can thank Mandy, honey. On the way to school, she

reminded me about the ice cream." He opened the second bag. "Now, I hope you ladies like steakburgers, fully loaded. If you don't like the pickles, just put them aside for Sam." He nodded toward his other cousin, who'd come out to greet him.

"I love pickles." Zoey accepted the burger he offered. "Thanks."

"Good." He glanced at Lauren with those brilliant blue eyes, and her pulse kicked up.

She quickly stuffed her silly reaction to his handsome appearance. "Why are you doing this?"

"Yeah, Cuz." Will returned from the back room and smirked at Robert. "Why are you feeding my employees?"

Lauren cringed inwardly. Couldn't her boss see the problem here? She hadn't dared to voice her dislike of Robert's intrusion into her and Zoey's lives, much less mention his hints that she'd lied about finding Lady. For all she knew, Will had no idea Robert had accused her of stealing the dog. Why not? She should be grateful that he hadn't already gotten her fired.

"Shouldn't you be out branding cattle or something?" Sam, who lived in one of the houses out at the ranch, leaned against the unfinished door frame. "What are you doing still in town?"

"My cattlemen's meeting lasted longer than expected. I figured if I was hungry, Zoey must be, too." Robert settled in a chair and pulled a wrapped burger from a bag. "You boys don't mind if I eat here, do you?"

"Make yourself at home," Will said. "I'll go get something for Sam and me." He left the office, grinning and shaking his head.

"Well, eat up, ladies." Robert unwrapped his burger.

"Mr. Mattson, we should thank the Lord for the food." Zoey hadn't even touched a French fry.

Robert gaped for a split second, then rewrapped his food. "Yes, ma'am. You're absolutely right." He closed his eyes. "Lord, thank You for this fine, sunny day. Thank You for

Your provision and for our good health. And thank You for the food. May it nourish our bodies to Your service. Amen."

"Amen." Zoey gave him a sweet smile as she picked up a French fry and gave Lauren an expectant look. "Dig in, Mom."

Lauren reluctantly unwrapped her burger and took a bite. Whatever sauce the restaurant used on their steakburgers made her mouth water in appreciation. The fries were thin, crisp and spicy. She looked at the logo on the bags. Mattsons' Steakhouse. Of course. The best and most expensive restaurant in Riverton. She'd planned to save up and take Zoey there one day.

How many other ways would this man interrupt her life and her plans before he left her alone?

Why had he brought lunch to Zoey and Lauren rather than just the ice cream he'd promised? Rob had no idea. As they ate in silence, he examined his actions. When he'd stopped by his family's restaurant for Zoey's promised ice cream, he'd decided to order a take-out burger. It only made sense to purchase one for the girl. And of course her mother.

He could see the distrust in Lauren's eyes. The suspicion about his motives. That made two of them. She'd voiced the question he still hadn't answered for himself—why was he doing this?

One glance at Zoey brought it all into focus. The kids. That was why. Bobby, Mandy and even Clementine had adopted Zoey, as Mandy put it, as a "sister of their hearts." For them, it was more than words. They lived it. When they weren't together at school, they FaceTimed on their phones, chatting about movies, music, even homework, as though they couldn't discuss all of that at school. She'd already helped Mandy improve her essay writing and taught Bobby some coding techniques his teacher didn't seem to know. And that was after just one week in the same classes.

If Zoey were a brat or had bad manners or if she looked down on his kids because she was smarter than they were, he might discourage their friendship. But she was a sweet little gal with a generous spirit and a great sense of humor, especially about her disability. Zoey could be pretty funny in her frank observations about any number of subjects. In the apparent absence of a father, she must have got those good qualities, not to mention her smarts, from her mother. Good thing Lauren hadn't passed on her tendency for untruths about Lady to her daughter.

He hadn't said anything to Will and Sam concerning his suspicions about their paralegal. Best not to until he had concrete evidence. He'd tried to call that Santa Fe vet to check her story about finding Lady, but the call went to voicemail, and he hadn't wanted to leave a message. Since then, he kept putting off a second attempt. Maybe it was an unconscious worry. Learning that his suspicions about Lauren's lack of integrity were right would mean he'd have to tell his cousins that their employee couldn't be trusted in the sensitive legal matters that comprised their business. Worse, he'd have to break off Zoey's friendship with his kids. It was hard enough to raise the twins without letting them hang out with bad influences, however passive or subtle they might be. Although he hadn't been able to put his decision into words as he bought their lunches, he knew deep down it was so he could spend time with Zoey to find out just how much she took after her mother.

If only women always told the truth. If only Jordyn had just admitted she was going behind his back that day...

He'd loved Jordyn with every part of his soul and being, and he knew she loved him just as much. But against his advice, against his *orders*, she'd been determined to train an untrustworthy horse. Years ago, his sister, Ashley, had disobeyed their dad and done the same thing, which was the reason Rob didn't want his wife to attempt it. At least Ashley's resulting broken back had healed, while Jordyn's bad fall killed her. In his experience, women did what they wanted, even going behind the backs of those who knew better, loved ones who only wanted to protect them from harm.

If only Lauren would just admit the truth.

By the end of the week, the doctor said Zoey could attend church on Sunday and school the following Tuesday, the day after Labor Day, although he advised against volleyball and horseback riding for several weeks. Lauren was glad not to be the one to forbid Zoey's activities. Her daughter definitely had a "get back on the horse" personality, which sometimes made it hard to protect her from possible injuries.

Despite last Sunday's unhappy ending, Lauren looked forward to church, where she enjoyed Pastor Tim's Bible-based sermon. After the morning service, people lingered on the church's front lawn, and Lauren spoke with several acquaintances she'd met through work. Out of the corner of her eye, she saw Zoey chatting with Mandy and Bobby, as though they hadn't seen her every day at the office when they brought Lady to keep her company. Those two kids were so special. Their genuine interest in Zoey almost made up for Robert's reserve. Almost. While he never failed to extend greetings to Zoey, the way he looked at Lauren always seemed to hold an accusation.

"Mom, Mom." Zoey hurried toward her with Mandy, Bobby and their grandmother close behind. "Mrs. Mattson wants us to come out to the ranch for a Labor Day barbecue. Can we go?"

Lauren cringed inwardly. "Oh, I don't know." She smiled at Andrea as she remembered their lovely chat on the Saturday before last when they'd first met. "Won't this be a family affair?"

Andrea laughed. "Well, yes and no. It's an informal Mattson reunion, so we have about sixty or seventy relatives and shirt-tail relatives come out to the ranch. But nobody checks your ID at the gate." She squeezed Lauren's hand. "Do say you'll come. I enjoyed our conversation when you came out last time. Unless you have other plans."

"Please say yes, Mom." Zoey's grin said she already knew the answer.

Lauren chuckled. "Yes, we'd love to come." With that many people and such a large ranch, she could easily avoid Robert. "What can I bring?"

"How about a relish tray?" Andrea said.

"Pickles, olives, that sort of thing?"

"Exactly."

"Great. I can do that."

At the grocery store on the way home, she and Zoey loaded up their cart with every possible pickled vegetable they could find, along with three divided plastic serving platters and plastic tongs. Their apartment fridge barely held everything they bought.

The next afternoon, they loaded up a cooler and drove to the Double Bar M Ranch. The closer they got, the bigger a knot grew in Lauren's stomach. What was she doing, going to Robert Mattson's home again? She must be out of her mind. Even in a large crowd, how would she manage to avoid him?

Chapter Six

Rob always enjoyed hosting the Labor Day family gathering. The family's long history in the area gave them friendships with many of their neighbors, but nothing was as satisfying as fellowship with family.

Twenty years ago, Dad had remodeled and modernized the two-story "big house," built in 1878, but he'd kept the antebellum look, with its white columned porch overlooking the Rio Grande. Other houses on the property gave evidence of the era in which they were built—a one-story brick ranch style, a two-story clapboard farmhouse, a sprawling adobe hacienda. Jordyn had called the ranch property an architectural crazy quilt.

Rob's cousin Andy, who was Sam's dad, lived in the farmhouse and always managed the barbecue pit. Today, as always, two sides of prime Mattson beef turned on a massive spit down by the barn. Mom had arranged for the countless dishes to be brought by other family members. Rob's only duty was to greet everybody and catch up on family news.

He knew Mom had invited Lauren and Zoey to come, but he still felt a kick under his ribs when the little gray Honda Fit pulled onto the property. Sam, who also lived in the farmhouse, was directing incoming traffic and pointed her to a parking spot by the white picket fence that surrounded the big house. When she stepped out of the little car wearing jeans and a frilly pink blouse, he felt another kick. Why did she have to look so pretty?

Before he could make his way over from the side porch to greet her, Mandy and Clementine ran to meet Zoey, with Lady scampering ahead of them. Zoey knelt and hugged the dog like she hadn't seen her just a few days ago. Rob hated to admit it, but Lady obviously favored Zoey. He released a sigh of annoyance. He never should have let Bobby talk him into taking Lady to the law office last week. It only reinforced their bond. Would the coming week on the cattle drive be enough to break it?

"Hey, Mr. Mattson." Zoey waved, a big smile on her sweet face.

As he approached the car, he returned a smile and touched the brim of his Stetson. "Hey, Zoey, Lauren. Welcome to the Double Bar M Ranch."

Lauren barely spared him a nod before moving toward the back of the car and opening the hatchback. To their credit, his daughters hurried to help her unload her cooler and bags.

"That's okay, girls," he said. "You and Zoey join the other kids." He tilted his head toward the informal soccer game being played in the north pasture. "I'll help Miss Lauren."

"Thanks, Dad." Mandy grabbed Zoey's hand and started in that direction.

"Hey, wait." Lauren set down her bag. "Zoey, you can't…"

Zoey rolled her eyes. "I know, Mom."

"Wear your helmet." Lauren held out the protective gear.

Zoey huffed out a big sigh but obeyed her mom. Poor kid. Helmet on and shoulders slumped, she walked away in her halting gait. Lady kept pace close beside her, but seemed careful not to trip her. As a growing puppy, the dog had "herded" the kids, especially Clementine, when they walked around the property. Now she seemed more companion than shepherd.

Once they got up in the mountains for the roundup, Rob would make sure she remembered her natural instincts.

He turned his attention back to Lauren. "Let me get that." He lifted the cooler. "How's she doing?" He pointed his chin toward the kids.

Lauren eyed him briefly before taking two canvas bags from the car and closing the hatchback. "She's fine."

"No seizures?"

Now Lauren gaped at him. "How do you know…?"

"I couldn't *not* hear your conversation with Doc Edwards at the ER last Sunday."

"Oh, right. You were hovering."

Not sure she was joking, he ignored her smirk. "I did a little reading up on the subject." He took a step toward the front lawn where he and his men had set up long tables in the shade of the cottonwood trees. "So, not everybody with CP has epileptic seizures, right? I'm sorry Zoey, and you of course, have to deal with that double problem. It must be a constant concern for you."

When she just stood there staring at him, he chuckled. "You coming?"

She shook her head but followed him through the open gate in the picket fence.

"Look, I just want my kids to understand CP and epilepsy so they can be sensitive to Zoey." Not entirely true. He was honestly concerned about the girl himself.

"That's very kind of you." There was a slight edge to her tone, but he couldn't decide whether it was irritation or something else.

Mom greeted Lauren with a hug, then helped her unpack. "This is amazing." She laughed. "Did you leave any pickles in the grocery store?"

"Tried not to." Lauren grinned.

No, not a grin. A genuine and very beautiful smile. For a

moment, Rob foolishly wished she would send that smile in his direction.

What was he thinking? He wasn't about to let this woman get under his skin. But as he watched her interacting so well with Mom and his other female relatives, he feared she already had.

Lauren had met a few of these ladies through Will and Sam, and today they welcomed her like an old friend. Everybody asked about Zoey.

"My niece is a senior." Sam's mother, Linda, was a graying, energetic woman in her early fifties. "When Zoey returns to school, Lizzie said she'll make sure Zoey's okay when they pass in the hallways between classes."

"Thanks." Lauren had to blink away a sudden tear. "All the kids have been so good to her."

"You seem surprised," Andrea said. "What was it like for her back home... Orlando, right?"

"Yes. Orlando." Lauren didn't want to talk about the cruel teasing Zoey had endured since kindergarten. "But this is home now."

Andrea eyed her for a moment before resuming her food arrangements. "Good." She placed protective net screens over the completed trays, then looked beyond Lauren. "Don't you have something to do?"

Lauren turned to see Robert leaning against a tree, arms crossed, a grin on his lips making the dimple on his cheek show up. Why was he hanging around? Did he worry she might steal a bite of food? Or commit some other dastardly deed? Every time he watched her, at church, at the hospital, at the law office, she felt a totally unfounded twinge of guilt.

The sound of an approaching vehicle caught Rob's attention, and he walked toward the newcomers. No longer under his scrutiny, Lauren relaxed and surveyed these beautiful surroundings. Early in her employment at the law office, Will had told her about the first Mattsons to settle here, a couple and their five sons, who arrived shortly after the Civil War. Unlike many cattle ranchers of those times, they'd weathered floods, bitter winters, cattle rustlers and numerous family tragedies to become an established force in the Riverton community. The story sounded like something out of one of those old-fashioned Western movies, with the "good guys" winning in the end.

Sam and Will were definitely good guys. She wasn't yet sure about Robert. At least where she was concerned. As much as she tried not to react, it stung her pride to have someone, especially a man of his prominence and apparent integrity, question her honesty. She'd gotten enough censure from her own family after her divorce, one of the reasons she'd moved so far from home.

An uproar erupted in the vicinity of the informal soccer field. Was that noise a cheer for a goal scored or alarm over an injury?

Zoey! Lauren didn't bother to excuse herself but dashed across the lawn and wide barnyard toward the sound. What was wrong with her that she forgot to watch her daughter? To her surprise, Robert was striding in that direction as well. They arrived at the fenced pasture at the same time.

As though they hadn't just given her a heart attack, the teens and young adults merrily went about their game, with Zoey cheering from outside the fence near the sidelines. Lauren slumped against the wooden railing beside her daughter and breathed out a quiet sigh.

"Good game?" Robert stood on Zoey's other side and bent to scratch Lady behind her ears.

"Yessir." Zoey grinned. "Bobby kicked a goal from over there." She pointed toward the middle of the field.

Robert focused on his son. "That far, eh? That's impressive."

Relieved that the uproar hadn't been about Zoey, Lauren yielded to the urge to tease him. "Wow. If he kicks that well, maybe he should play soccer instead of football. I mean, if *family tradition* isn't allowed to override talent." And expectations.

Robert snorted. "Yeah, right. That'll be the day."

Zoey looked at him, then at Lauren. A sly grin appeared on her lips, and one eyebrow shot up. Lauren frowned and shook her head. Her daughter had never been a matchmaker, so this was new. Lauren would have to stop that thinking before it gained traction.

The ringing clatter of an old-fashioned triangle dinner bell sounded loudly across the ranch.

"About time." Robert chuckled. "That's Andy announcing the meat's ready." He lifted a hand to his mouth and called out to the soccer players. "Head for the chuckwagon, cowboys. Time to eat."

As the fifteen or sixteen young people raced toward the barn, whooping and laughing as they ran, Lauren felt an odd little thrill, but not because she was hungry. This must have been what it was like back in the olden days. She could picture all the ladies in their bonnets and long dresses. As for the men, they'd probably dressed much like their descendants did now—jeans, checkered shirts and Stetson hats. The presence of the many pickup trucks, especially Robert's monster black truck, confirmed the setting was now instead of then.

Guests poured from every part of the ranch and hurried toward the feast. Once the crowd had gathered under the cottonwood trees, Robert put his fingers to his lips and sent out a piercing whistle to get everyone's attention. "All right, y'all, quiet down. Cousin Rev came all the way down from his church up in Alamosa to bless the food, so bow your heads."

While the minister offered a lovely prayer, Lauren tried her best to keep her head lowered. But something urged her to look up, only to find Robert watching her. Why did he keep doing that? Should she leave? No. That would break Zoey's heart. Might as well just try to stay away from him and enjoy the day as much as she could.

With lively country tunes wafting in the air through an outdoor sound system, enjoying herself wasn't hard to do. She'd always preferred country music, one of the many things Singleton had criticized. As his wife, she'd been required to attend highbrow theater events and even opera. But the folksy, down-to-earth sound of country spoke to her soul in ways that even a gifted tenor singing a high C never could.

She helped Zoey fill her plate and sat across from Andrea at one of the many long tables. At the first bite, she closed her eyes and savored the tender beef. "Andrea, this is the best barbecue I've ever tasted."

"It sure is." Andrea laughed. "Since I didn't fix it, I don't mind accepting compliments for my nephew."

"Hey, Lauren." Sam brought his plate and sat next to her. "Cover for me, will you? Ever since Will got married, he's been trying to line me up with a girlfriend. If I'm with you, maybe he and his latest pick will leave me alone."

"Sure, boss. Glad to help." Lauren covered her amusement by taking a bite of coleslaw. Sam was young enough not to realize he'd given her a backhanded compliment.

"Sam, I'm ashamed of you." Andrea scowled at him across the table. "Lauren, you must excuse this rude boy. He should be downright happy to be in the company of a pretty girl like you." She waved a scolding finger at Sam. "And happy to have you working for him. I'm sure you keep those boys in line at the office."

As Lauren tried to think of a humorous quip, a large presence hovered over her like a shadow of doom.

"Mind if I sit here?" Robert didn't wait for an answer, but

stepped over the bench and plunked himself down on Zoey's other side. So much for avoiding him.

"Son, do you think there's enough food for everybody?" Andrea glanced around the crowd. "Maybe Andy should have cooked three sides of beef."

"Mom, you know that's never a problem." Robert cut into his juicy slab of meat. "And we always have plenty of leftovers to take to the church outreach program."

"That's very generous. Most people would tuck away leftovers to feast on for days." Once again, Lauren found something to respect about Robert Mattson. Or at least his family.

And once again, Zoey cast a teasing look at her, adding a nudge with her elbow. When they got home, Lauren would have to sit her daughter down and tell her to stop it.

Rob made sure the band was fed before they set up in the barn. It wouldn't be Labor Day at the Double Bar M Ranch without a good old-fashioned barn dance. Once they started the live music, nobody had to make an announcement. Family and guests crowded the wide aisles of the largest barn to show off their footwork in line dancing, square dancing, even the lively polka Mom had insisted on. Boot scooting in a line dance was more his speed.

When "Achy Breaky Heart" began, somehow he ended up next to Lauren in the second row of dancers. While many folks had begun to wilt by the end of this hot day, Lauren looked as fresh as she had when she stepped out of her car this afternoon. And pretty cute as she struggled to keep up with the tricky moves of the dance. When she bumped into him for the second time, he could see from her shocked expression that she hadn't meant to.

"Sorry." Her face reddened as she stood watching the footwork of the front line, then shook her head. "Nope. Can't do it." She started to move past him.

Without thinking, he touched her arm. "Hey, don't give up."

Blinking her gray-green eyes, she looked up at him, and an odd feeling skittered through him. *Man*, she sure was pretty. *Quit that!*

"Come on, now." He took her hand. "Follow me." He waited for the right beat of the music. "Four steps to the right. Four steps to the left." Gripping his hand, she managed to follow him. "Now heel touches. One, two, three, four. Now four steps to face the right."

As they continued each different movement, her grip loosened, and she seemed to catch on. By the time the song ended, she was smiling.

"That was fun, but I don't think sneakers are made for line dancing." She applauded with the rest of the crowd. "Maybe if I get some Western boots, I'll do better next time."

As she moved away from him, he argued with himself over asking her to dance with him for the next number, a country-western waltz. Being the main host of this shindig, he should also ask other ladies to dance. He hesitated about one second too long. Sam approached her and gave a comical bow.

"Miz Parker, may I have this dance?"

"Why, yes, Mr. Mattson, you may." She took his hand and followed him back to the floor without a backward glance.

Rob stared after them. Was his young cousin falling for his paralegal? After all, he'd sought her out during dinner even though she was somewhere in her late thirties, at least ten years older than Sam. Then Rob saw Will glaring at the couple. Oh, right. Will was trying to set Sam up with the neighbor lady who stood beside him. Rob snorted out a laugh. Since he'd danced with Lauren, maybe his young cousin would consider that particular matchmaking job a success and would leave him alone. Never mind that Rob had no interest in taking up with any woman, especially Lauren Parker. But just in case

Will needed more proof of his supposed success, Rob would be sure to ask her to dance at least one more time.

"Mom, that was so much fun." Zoey sat on her bed brushing her long brown hair. "I just love going out to the ranch." Even though she hadn't tried to dance, she'd enjoyed talking with the other teens. And the entire day, Lady never left her side. Had even tried to get into the car when they were leaving, much to Robert's obvious annoyance. "Can we do it again?"

"Sure. If we're invited." Lauren didn't want to remind her daughter that the riding lessons would have to wait until the doctor gave her the all clear. She also didn't want to mention that Robert treated her with suspicion when no one else was looking. Yes, he'd danced with her twice, the line dance and the last-call slow two-step. But the openness he displayed when talking to his other guests dissolved into a cool reserve when he spoke to her.

"Time for bed, sweetheart. Busy school day tomorrow."

At work the next morning, it seemed odd not to have Zoey *and* Lady on a cot behind her desk. It also seemed odd not to have Robert and his kids bring the dog and come get her after school. She should have been glad not to have interruptions to her work, but she had to admit the addition of a social life felt good. Yesterday she'd made some new friends whose warm welcomes made up for Robert's reserve, at least a little.

"So, Miz Parker." Will set a document on her desk. "Did you enjoy dancing with Big Boss?"

She gave him an innocent blink. "Who? Oh, yes. Robert was very helpful with the line dancing, but I really enjoyed the waltz with Sam. He sure can dance up a storm. Maybe it's the cowboy boots. My sneakers weren't the best shoes to wear."

Will chuckled. "Right. Okay, back to work. Can you input these adoption papers for me and print out four copies? Judge Mathis will sign them on Thursday."

"No problem." She checked his notes to be sure they were legible, then got to work.

At noon, she saw Robert's huge black truck roll by and feared…hoped?…for a moment he would stop by. Why did she want to see him again? Did she somehow hope to prove him wrong about her? How foolish and useless. She'd spent three years trying to please Singleton, but he always found something to criticize. Besides, she had nothing to prove to Robert.

Due to the noontime Main Street traffic, he drove slowly, so she was able to read the new addition to the large truck. "Double Bar M Ranch" had been painted on the door, with his own name underneath in smaller letters. Did he drive that huge truck through town to show off how wealthy he was?

Oh, dear. Now who was judging? As much as his attitude toward her made her uncomfortable, she hadn't observed any overblown pride. Or maybe he was just good at hiding it. Not that she cared to find out, but working for his cousins, and their kids being friends, how could she manage to avoid the man?

Worse still, deep inside, did she even really want to avoid him?

Chapter Seven

❧

"But why do I have to go on roundup, Dad?" Bobby came close to pouting like he used to do as a three-year-old. "I hate to miss my classes. What about my grades? My programming club?"

"Come on, now." Rob noticed his son hadn't mentioned missing a week's worth of football practice. "Be honest. You'll miss your friends more than your classes." He took a bite of Mom's amazing meatloaf, then waved his fork at Bobby. "I've told you before, there's more to your education than what you learn in the schoolroom. I should've taken you with me last April when we trucked the cattle up to summer pasture. Now, no more arguments. You're going with me this Saturday because you need to see that side of ranching. Remember, these are things you need to know for the day when you'll manage this ranch."

Bobby rolled his eyes. "How could I forget?" He bent over his plate, shoulders hunched. Beside him, Lady laid her head on his knee, and he absentmindedly petted her.

What was wrong with this boy? In his own younger years, Rob had ached for the day when he went on his first roundup. When Dad had finally let him go at fourteen, he'd had the time of his life. It wasn't like Bobby was lazy or scared. He did his barn chores without complaint and rode like a champ... though he didn't care about signing up for rodeo events. But then, not every cowboy felt the need to compete in the arena.

"Dad, if you need another hand," Mandy said, "I could go instead of Bobby. I want to learn how to do the hard stuff." She blinked those blue eyes at him, which usually made him cave. Not this time.

"Me too," Clementine piped up, her expression as hopeful as Mandy's.

"Thanks, girls. You just take care of your schoolwork. That's your job."

They ate in silence until Bobby spoke up again.

"I've got a great idea, Dad." His grin warned Rob that he wasn't going to like whatever bright idea this was. "I won't argue about going with you if you let me take my tablet so I can keep up with my assignments, and—" he gave Mandy a conspiratorial wink "—if you leave Lady with Zoey while we're gone." Lying on the floor beside his chair, the dog lifted her head at the mention of her name.

"What?" Rob thought his head might explode. "Where do you get these ideas? Lady is your dog, and she's going on the roundup with us so she can reconnect with her herding instincts and remember her early training."

"But—"

"No!" Rob slapped his hand on the table, rattling the silverware and sloshing the iced tea in his glass. Clementine looked like she was about to cry, and Mandy ducked her head. Bobby just glared at him.

"Robert…" Mom stared at him with the look that still could give him pause.

He exhaled a slow breath. "Look, son, I carefully chose Lady from an exceptional litter, and I spent over two thousand dollars for her. She's an investment in the future. Your future. And her job is to herd cattle and teach her future pups to do the same. This Saturday, she's going on roundup with us."

As he spoke, Lady watched his face. To her credit, she hadn't jumped at his outburst. That proved she hadn't lost the shockproof instincts she'd displayed as a puppy that caused him to choose her out of a litter of five.

"You can take your tablet and work on your assignments in the evenings. If I need to write a note to your teachers, I'll do it. Most of them understand that big ranches around here, including the Double Bar M, go on roundup every September, and they've always made allowances for it."

And what was this about wanting Zoey to keep Lady while they were gone? Even if Rob let her stay home, Mandy was perfectly capable of tending her. No need to bother Lauren by adding dog care on top of her full-time job.

Against his better thinking, a picture of the honey-brown-haired beauty flashed into his mind. When he'd driven down Main Street one day last week, he'd noticed her through the storefront glass of the law office. If he wasn't mistaken, she saw him, too. It had given him that ridiculous kick under his ribs he often felt around her. Yes, she was pretty, but she always seemed to watch him warily, as if she knew one day he would uncover the truth about how she "found" Lady. Maybe when he got back from roundup, he could finally reach that Santa Fe vet.

Why was he putting off trying to call him again? Maybe he didn't really want to know the truth. If she was responsible for Lady being stolen, he'd have to have her arrested, which would lead to problems for Zoey. But if Lauren was as innocent as the look in her soulful eyes seemed to indicate, he just might be the one with a problem. Since Jordyn's death, he hadn't felt the slightest interest in any woman, no matter how much matchmaking Will did or how many women at church tried to get his attention. Then this woman barges into his life, and he can't stop thinking about her. What was wrong with him? Hopefully, nothing that a week of rounding up cattle couldn't cure.

* * *

Lauren didn't know why Mandy had invited Zoey out to the ranch. With laundry and housecleaning to do, she hated giving up another Saturday. But she wouldn't deny Zoey the opportunity to watch the cowboys load up their trucks and drive off to their roundup. She wouldn't mind seeing it herself, like observing a real-life version of the old Westerns her dad liked to watch on television.

As Mandy advised in last night's text, they arrived at the Double Bar M Ranch shortly after dawn to observe all the action. Even before parking, she saw Robert directing his ranch hands as they loaded eight horses into the long trailer attached to the back of his huge black truck. That answered her question about why he needed such a monster vehicle. She hadn't even tried to pull a small U-Haul with her little car, but had shipped their few household goods to their new home. She couldn't imagine the power needed to pull a loaded horse trailer up into the mountains.

With a lot of action happening around the barn, she parked near the picket fence by the main house. Zoey was out of the car before Lauren shut off the motor.

"Zoey, wait." She ran around the car to catch her daughter. To her surprise, Zoey was kneeling with Lady in her arms while the dog licked her face. A leash hung from her collar.

The other two dogs trotted over to greet them, but Bobby called to them, and they raced back to the trailer. Lady stayed with Zoey.

Lauren waved to Andrea and Linda, who were packing another large pickup with boxes and coolers, probably the provisions for the cowboys. Nearby, Bobby lifted a saddle into the horse trailer's front storage area, and Mandy handed him some other tack.

"Mom, it's so exciting." Zoey's eyes sparkled.

Feeling the excitement herself, Lauren smiled. "It sure is,

sweetie." As before, she marveled at all the work it took so that people could have steaks and hamburgers and leather purses. And fancy Western boots, of course.

Mandy hurried over and grabbed Lady's leash. "Silly girl. How'd you get away from me?" She gave Zoey a hug. "Hi, Mrs. Parker." A hint of sadness clouded her face.

"Hi, Mandy. Are you okay?" Lauren had never seen this girl without a smile.

Mandy sighed. "Dad's making Bobby go on the roundup, but he won't let me go."

"I wish I could go," Zoey laughed. "But I guess I'd just get in the way." She eyed Mandy. "But you wouldn't get in the way. You'd know what to do, right?"

Mandy sighed again. "Yeah, but Dad doesn't see it that way. He never lets me do any of the hard stuff around the ranch. He's so unfair to me."

"I think it's more than that." Why was Lauren defending Robert? Maybe because she understood it wasn't easy to be a parent. She often had a hard time letting Zoey do challenging activities, such as riding a horse. Or playing volleyball. But while kids should experience new things as they matured, a caring parent knew what his or her child needed. "He's just looking out for you."

"Humph." Mandy reached down and petted Lady. "Zoey, did you ask your mom about keeping Lady for us?"

"What? When did this happen?" Lauren stared at the two girls.

Zoey grinned. "In her text last night. That's why she invited us to come out this morning."

"Well, aren't you two sneaky?" Lauren crossed her arms. "Why isn't she going on the roundup?" She couldn't imagine Robert doing this, not when he still thought she had something to do with Lady's theft. "Wasn't he planning to teach her how to herd cattle?"

"Seems the Lord had a different plan." Mandy glanced toward the busy barnyard, where Robert now strode toward them. "Last night we discovered Lady needs to be kept inside for a while so she doesn't run off and find herself another, shall we say, *inappropriate* boyfriend." She and Zoey giggled. "That's why we have her on the leash, so she can't run away."

As this revelation began to make sense to Lauren, Robert reached them.

"Can you handle this?" His gruff tone underscored his cross expression. "This was a last-minute thing, so—"

"Yes, I'm happy to help. But—" She should ask why Lady couldn't just stay on the ranch, but the hopeful look in Zoey's eyes stopped her.

"Good. Just keep her indoors except for morning and evening walks, and be sure you hold on tight to that leash. She'll be all right alone in your apartment during the day. Also, my cousin Sue is a vet, and she can answer any questions and give you any supplies at my expense." He handed Lauren a business card. "Give her a call."

The way he spoke to her, he was clearly used to giving orders to anybody and everybody and expecting them to obey. She wanted to salute and say, *Aye, aye, sir.* Good sense kept her right hand at her side. Never mind that she and Zoey had taken good care of Lady all summer. "I can do that."

He stared at her. "Yes, I'm sure you can. Mandy, you take care of your sister and grandma while we're gone." He spun around on his dusty cowboy boots and strode away like the Big Boss that he was. An old-fashioned movie hero couldn't have done it any better.

Lauren watched him, her emotions hovering between admiration for the attractive man and annoyance at his high-handed ways. She shook away those thoughts and turned to Mandy. "We're happy to take care of Lady for you, but why can't she just stay here in your house?"

"Mom!" Zoey protested.

Mandy just shrugged. "Have you ever seen my little sister close the door when she goes outside? Never. When we noticed Lady's condition last evening, Dad thought…well, he agreed with Bobby and me…that she'd make a run for it and get into trouble again. The best solution was to ask Zoey, and you of course, to make sure she's safe and happy." She petted Lady. "Just so you know, Bobby and I and even Clementine can see Lady loves Zoey and wants to be with her."

Lauren resisted agreeing with her, at least in Zoey's hearing. "How do you feel about that?"

Mandy's smile was genuine. "We agree. We love her, of course, but we aren't very attached to her. Besides, we have the other dogs." She laughed. "And more cats than you can count."

Lauren didn't know what to say. Should she offer to buy Lady? No, she couldn't afford such a pricey pet. Besides, she doubted Robert would sell her his expensive breeding dog. It was a wonder he'd allowed Zoey to keep her, but then, he'd been forced to by Lady's unexpected condition. She hadn't been back with the Mattsons long enough for them to predict it.

The sun rose above the horizon as Robert's monster truck rolled past her pulling the loaded horse trailer. He glanced her way and touched the brim of his hat, cowboy gentleman that he was, but didn't smile. Not that he'd ever actually smiled at her. But it wasn't her fault he'd made the decision to let her, well, *Zoey* take care of Lady while he took care of ranch business.

She'd always thought no man could be as controlling and annoying as her ex-husband. But Robert Mattson had Singleton beat by a mile.

Rob inhaled a lungful of pure, icy mountain air, sensing the imminence of an early winter. He nestled down into his sleeping bag, pleased this roundup was going so well. Back in

1888 and again in 1923, his family had lost much of their herd in early winter storms. After those disasters, they'd learned to read the signs about when to get their steers to market.

He looked up at the countless stars dotting the blackened sky and whispered, "Thank You, Lord, for all of this beauty. For the ranch. For a healthy herd. For my family."

He glanced toward the one-man tent where Bobby sat hunched over his tablet. How could that kid prefer to stare at a screen instead of enjoying the untamed wilderness pastures that would one day belong to him? This week, he'd done a decent job of scouting out some mavericks under Andy's guidance and with the help of Irish and Scotch. Did he enjoy working with the dogs? Had he caught the cowboy bug yet? If his hurry to get back to his tablet was any indication, the answer was no.

How could he have spent his entire fifteen years on the ranch without loving this life? How many kids his age got to spend the night under the stars and know the satisfaction of a job well done? Some of Rob's best talks with his dad had been right here in these mountains during roundup. The memory gave him an idea.

"Hey, Bobby."

No answer.

"Bobby!"

"Yessir?" The mumbled response revealed his preoccupation.

"Come on out here."

His sigh was deep and audible. "Yessir."

His tablet light went out, and he crawled out of the shelter he preferred to the open air, pulling a blanket around his shoulders and shuddering.

"You need something, Dad?"

Rob was thankful Bobby couldn't see the annoyance that must be written across his face. "Yeah. Go make sure Scotch

and Irish have enough water in their pan." The two border collies had worked hard today, although before they left home, it
had been tricky to keep Scotch away from Lady.

"I already did."

"Good. Now come over here and sit with me." Rob pulled
himself up and crossed his legs. "So, what did you learn today?"

Bobby plunked down on the edge of the sleeping bag. "It's
really cool, Dad. I figured out a really cool coding sequence
that will help my programming team when we compete in Albuquerque in November." The excitement in his voice gave
Rob a chill that was anything but "really cool."

"Good. I'm glad you're doing so well. But how about the
roundup? Did Uncle Andy have some good things to teach
you?"

"Yessir." Bobby glanced back at his tent. Even in the dim
light of the campfire, Rob could see his longing to get back
to his tablet.

"Like what?"

Bobby sighed…again. "Well, he showed me how Scotch
and Irish use teamwork to herd the steers and how they know
which ones of the new calves belongs to which mother and
how to keep them together."

"Right." This was good. How could he keep it going? "And
Lady will do the same thing once she's back in training. She's
got the right instincts. We just need to work with her a little
more."

Bobby stared at him for a few seconds. "I don't want to say
you're wrong, Dad, but—"

"But you think I'm wrong."

Bobby grinned. "Yessir."

Now Rob sighed. "Yeah, well, I paid too much for her to
give up and let her be somebody's pet." Annoyance threaded
through his chest over being trapped into letting Lady stay
with Zoey and Lauren. But he'd had no choice. Six days ago,

they had to get on the road before sunup, so he didn't have time to figure out another plan. With time, he'd have boarded her at Cousin Sue's vet clinic. Too many last-minute decisions prevented that.

Would Zoey be able to keep Lady indoors? Would they be able to hang on to her leash when they took her out for her walks? Despite his suspicions about Lauren, he had to admit she was a responsible person, although her wary expression when she looked at him kept his suspicions alive.

Why did he spend so much time thinking about that frustrating woman? And why hadn't he just tried to call the Santa Fe vet again to find out the truth?

Simple. He didn't want to know. Feeding his suspicions helped him keep a wall between them, one that those pretty gray-green eyes might just one day pierce through his resolve like a laser beam. And at all cost, he had to prevent that.

Chapter Eight

Lauren didn't usually watch the clock, but today she fidgeted in her chair as quitting time neared. Yesterday evening, Robert had texted his plan to come by the apartment this evening to take Lady home. Lauren had mixed feelings about seeing him again. Would he be his usual gruff self, or would he show some gratitude to Zoey at least for taking care of Lady? With that man, she could never guess.

Finally the hands of the antique clock above the door reached five and twelve. Lauren saved her document, closed out the program and logged off of her computer.

"Any plans for tonight?" Will asked Sam as they emerged from the back offices.

"Um, well…"

"Why don't you come out to our place and finally meet the young lady who's renting our art studio? She's—"

"Lauren!" Sam's voice held a hint of panic. "Don't you still need me to hang that shadow box for you?"

She managed not to laugh. Should she encourage Will's matchmaking or rescue Sam from his cousin's plans? In fact, it might be good to have him at the apartment when Robert arrived.

"I hate to spoil your fun, Will, but I keep tripping over the shadow box. It sure would be nice to have it on the wall and out of the way."

He gave her a skeptical smirk. "Yeah, right." He clapped Sam on the shoulder. "Don't think you're going to get out of meeting Lily. She's—"

"Will you look at the time." Sam glanced at his watch. "Lauren, I'll be right over after I grab supper."

"Why not eat with Zoey and me? We're having spaghetti."

Eyes narrowed, Will looked back and forth between them with fake annoyance. "Okay. Have it your way." He plopped his Stetson on his head and walked to the door. "See you two at church on Sunday. Don't forget to lock up."

As he made his exit, Lauren grabbed her purse. "You don't really have to be my personal handyman, Sam. If you have Friday night plans, feel free to change your mind."

"Ha. After you saved me from the clutches of some artsy type woman Will and Olivia think is *just perfect* for me?" He snorted. "And this coming from the guy who resisted romance even when it smacked him in the face. No, I'm more than happy to help you out."

"Okay, then." Back in Orlando, Lauren had managed to avoid several matchmaking attempts herself. Thankfully, no one here in Riverton had signed up for that job. "See you at my place in a few."

The ten-block drive to her apartment complex took longer than usual due to Friday evening traffic. Lauren pulled into her designated parking space and hurried into the building a little breathless. She was met by Mrs. Walston, the neighbor who checked on Zoey every day.

"All's quiet on the Western Front," the retired history teacher said. "I watched as she walked that pretty little dog down to the end of the block and back again."

"Thank you." Lauren hesitated before adding, "I have a guest…two guests coming over this evening. My boss and the man who owns Lady." As kind as Mrs. Walston was, she did have a tendency to gossip, not to mention to go on and on about random topics, so it was best to keep her informed. It was a small thing to put up with her borderline snooping to have a responsible adult who cared enough to keep an eye on Zoey when Lauren was at work.

"How nice." The lady gave her a maternal smile. "Well, you enjoy your evening." She disappeared behind her door.

Entering her own first-floor apartment, Lauren was greeted by a wagging dog and the aroma of onions cooking. She knelt to ruffle Lady's fur and accepted her welcome-home licks, then they both joined Zoey in the kitchen. "I see you've started supper."

"Yep." Zoey beamed with self-confidence. "I'm getting ready to brown the hamburger." She was struggling to pull apart the edges of the package of grain-fed ground beef.

"Here. Let me." Lauren reached for the meat.

Zoey turned one shoulder. "I can do it."

"Right." Letting her daughter struggle was the hardest part of parenting. "I have trouble separating the sides, too. I usually give up and use the scissors."

Zoey rolled her eyes. "Okay. I can take a hint." She took the scissors from the knife block and struggled to cut into the plastic wrap.

Nearby, Lady watched Zoey, tilting her head as though questioning what she was doing. When the scissors slipped from her wet hands, Lauren gasped softly, and Lady let out a little whimper.

"Okay, you guys, stop that." Zoey speared each of them with a cross look before trying again. This time, the sharp blades crosscut through the plastic, and she was able to pull the meat out and place it in the sizzling pan of onions. Only a little grease popped up. "See. I can do it."

"Yes, you can." Lauren gave her a side hug. "Since you have this all in hand, what can I do to help?"

"Make the salad." Zoey reached into the skillet, carefully

pinched off a tiny piece of hamburger and held it out to Lady. The grateful dog licked it from her hand and seemed to smile. Zoey stepped over to the sink and washed her hands, then returned to the stove to break up the meat with a cooking spoon. "Mom? Salad?"

Lauren resisted the urge to suggest a different tool. "Right." She opened the fridge. "Hey, you remember Mandy's dad is coming to pick up Lady?"

Zoey stabbed at the meat. "I remember."

"And Sam's coming over to hang the shadow box, so I invited him to eat with us."

"For supper?" Zoey stared at her, panic in her eyes. "Mom, you take over here." She held out the spoon. "I don't want you to get fired for serving your boss lumpy spaghetti sauce."

"I'm sure he won't fire me for that, but maybe for not having dessert." Lauren accepted the spoon and set it in the sink, then selected the four-bladed meat chopper from the utensil holder and began to break the hamburger into small bits. "How about you whip up some peach cobbler?"

While her daughter assembled the canned peaches and biscuit mix, Lauren filled a stockpot with water and turned on the back burner. A knock sounded on the door just as Zoey put the cobbler in the oven. She hurried to answer, with Lady close beside her.

"I hope you don't mind," Sam said as they entered the kitchen. "I brought my checkers and board to teach Zoey. We talked about it the other week when she was at the office. Is that okay?" Like his cousin Will, and unlike his cousin Robert, Sam had a relaxed, personable way about him. Once Robert took Lady later this evening, it would be good to have something to distract Zoey.

"Sounds good." He might be her boss, but Lauren was still in charge here at home. "Zoey, how's your homework coming?"

"No problem." She grinned. "I finished most of it in study hall."

"Then checkers it is."

While she and Zoey finished supper preparations, Sam mounted the heavy shadow box over the chest of drawers in Zoey's bedroom.

Lauren spread a tablecloth over the battered card table they used for dining, then set up three metal folding chairs. Sam didn't seem to mind bending his tall frame into the chair. At Lauren's invitation, he offered a blessing for the food and added a request for Lady to have an easy transition back to the ranch. Lauren sent him a grateful smile. He and Will hadn't taken sides about the dog, but they seemed to know all about it and still hadn't fired her. Maybe Robert hadn't told them of his suspicions.

"That's quite a collection of doodads you've got in your shadow box, Zoey," Sam said. "Where'd you get all that stuff?" He twirled a bite of spaghetti onto his fork and put it in his mouth.

"We collected them at the truck stops as we drove across the country." Zoey had been proud of the various tiny figurines she'd found. "They're reminders of where we've traveled."

They were halfway into dessert when another knock sounded on the door.

"I'll get it." Sam rose from the table and headed toward the door before Lauren could move. "Hey, Rob."

Lauren had to smother a laugh at the surprised expression on Robert's face.

"Sam." Robert entered and removed his hat. "What're you doing here?"

"Just helping Lauren out and honing my handyman skills. Come on in. I'm sure there's enough of Zoey's peach cobbler for you to join us."

Lauren wanted to punch her boss's arm. What was he doing

by playing the part of host? Even so, she quickly laid out a place mat for Robert and unfolded another chair. "Yes, come have a seat. You're just in time. I'm not sure Sam planned to leave any cobbler or ice cream."

Lady wandered over to greet Robert, then returned to her spot beside Zoey's chair. Lauren swallowed the sudden emotion trying to rise in her throat. She would miss Lady almost as much as Zoey. Almost, but not quite. Zoey's eyes glistened with tears, but she managed to smile. After their guests left, they would have a good cry together.

"This is mighty tasty, Zoey. I sure wasn't expecting this." Rob had been raised never to turn down an offered dessert. Mom insisted a hardworking man could always find room for a lady's homemade specialty, no matter how it tasted, as a goodwill gesture. In this case, Zoey's cobbler was almost as good as Mom's, though he thought maybe she'd used store-bought canned peaches and a biscuit mix, while Mom made hers with home-canned peaches and scratch dough. "Thanks."

"You're welcome. And thank you for letting us take care of Lady." Zoey's eyes seemed a bit teary. No surprise there. "We kept her indoors except for her walks, just like you said. She was used to being here, so I think that's why she didn't try to get away. One time on our walk, when I was daydreaming about my homework and stepped into the street, she pulled me back before a car came zooming past us." She reached down and petted Lady. "I guess she was herding me back to safety." She laughed softly, and her voice broke. Was it from emotion or due to her CP?

Rob grimaced, imagining the dangerous scene. "I don't know which to comment on first. She sure was doing a good job of watching out for you." He chuckled. "But you were actually daydreaming about homework?"

Sam also chuckled, while Lauren sent Rob a grateful smile—a smile he felt deep in his chest.

Zoey rolled her eyes at his teasing, just like Mandy always did. "Yes. I have to write a short story for English class, and I'm writing about how we found Lady. That takes a lot of planning so I can make it interesting."

Rob glanced at Lauren, who ducked her head. Guilt? Would Zoey's school assignment finally reveal the truth about how Lady came into their lives? He doubted the girl would lie, but she might make up a fictional version of the events. "I'd like to read that when you're done."

"Sure." Zoey grinned. "I'd like that."

"And on that note—" He reached into his back pocket and took out his wallet. "We didn't discuss your dog-watching fee. Would a hundred—"

"Absolutely not." Lauren glared at him, then softened her look. "We were happy to help out in a pinch. And Lady was a perfect…well, lady. It was a pure pleasure to watch her. Besides, you don't charge us for Zoey's riding lessons."

At the finality in her tone, he put the wallet away. He noticed she didn't say they'd missed Lady living with them or repeat what Zoey said about the dog feeling right at home here. He had to give her credit for that.

"Okay. Thanks." He noticed Zoey's sweet smile, so apparently she agreed with her mom. "So, when are you coming back out to ride?" What was he saying? He didn't usually speak without thinking, but this time his tongue seemed to have a mind of its own.

"Doc says give it another week, and if I take my meds and don't have any seizures, I can ride a week from tomorrow. I can't wait."

The eagerness in her voice made him smile. "Great. I'll tell the kids, and we'll plan on it."

"In the meantime," Sam said, "let's exercise your strategizing skills with a good game of checkers."

While they talked checkers, Rob took the opportunity to glance around the apartment. The kitchen was a small alcove off of the living and dining areas. Down the short hallway, he could see two open bedroom doors. In the living area, a small flat-screen television sat on a low table across from two well-worn upholstered chairs. On the walls were a couple of stock photo pictures and two homemade cross-stitch samplers of Bible verses. This rickety old card table looked like it came from the 1800s.

Life couldn't be easy for this mom. Zoey wore T-shirts and ripped jeans like the other kids, while Lauren wore the same navy pantsuit he'd seen her wearing at work when he'd brought them lunch. Was that her only professional clothing? They didn't appear to have much in the way of material things, but the room felt like it was filled with love. Truth was, he had to respect that, especially since she'd refused the money he'd tried to offer. He wasn't about to spoil these impressions by trying again to reach that Santa Fe vet. At least not yet.

"Thanks for the dessert." He carefully pushed the uncomfortable metal chair back from the wobbly table. "Time for me to collect my dog and head out." He bent down and ruffled Lady's fur behind her ears. "Come on, girl. Let's go home." He gripped her collar and tugged, only to have her resist his efforts by settling firmly on the floor and whining. Smart dog. She knew what this was about.

Zoey reached down to pet her. "You do what he says, Lady. It's time for you to go home."

Again her eyes…and Lauren's…shone with tears. Rob had to grip his own emotions. "Come on, girl." He lifted Lady and headed toward the door, with Sam following. "You coming?"

"Nope. Just want to tell you something. Like I said, Zoey and I are going to play checkers." Sam followed Rob out of the apartment. "That week Zoey spent at the office gave Will and me a chance to notice how she blossoms with some brotherly, or *uncle-ly*, if that's a word, attention. That's why I thought she might like checkers." He turned away, then back again. "Lauren's a nice lady. You should take her out." He nudged Rob's arm and grinned, then stepped back into the apartment. "See you, Cuz."

Rob shook off his annoyance at Sam's suggestion. As he headed toward his truck, Lady whimpered and wiggled in his arms. Once in the vehicle, she slumped down on the seat, apparently resigned. Her condition had changed, so after he drove through the ranch's front gate, he let her run free. She greeted Scotch and Irish, then followed him into the house.

"Lady!" Clementine greeted them at the door and knelt to give the dog a hug. "Welcome home." Lady licked her face and leaned into the hug. Rob figured Clementine was the dog's second favorite person in the world after Zoey. What would it take for her loyalty to transfer back to Bobby?

Bobby wandered into the front hall munching on one of Mom's giant blueberry muffins. "Hey, Lady." He petted her, then headed for the staircase.

"Hey." Rob couldn't keep the sharp tone from his voice. "This is your dog. You need to keep her with you."

"Oh." Bobby blinked in that "is anybody home" way of his. "Yeah. Come on, Lady."

She looked between him and Clementine and plodded after him with obvious reluctance.

Rob released a long sigh. How was he going to get a return on the investment he'd made in this valuable dog when his son couldn't care less about training her? Worse than that, how could he get his son interested in his own inheritance? Since the late 1880s, five generations of Robert Mattsons had owned and managed the Double Bar M Ranch. It was a hands-on operation, but with Bobby's interest focused on computers and electronics, he'd probably try texting orders to his cowhands. Yeah, that would work for maintaining a healthy herd of cattle. Not.

Rob didn't usually have trouble sleeping, but he lay awake far into the night worrying about his legacy and feeling like he'd somehow failed his ancestors. Lauren's pretty face and the one real smile she'd sent his way that evening came to mind. She had single-parent worries, too. How did she cope with the challenges life threw her way? At least Rob didn't have to worry about providing for his family.

One of the samplers on her wall read, "Trust in the Lord with all thine heart."

Maybe that was how she did it, by trusting in the Lord. When he was younger and life was easier, he'd always believed God had his life under control. Then Jordyn died, and his faith had taken a hit. Maybe it was time to try trusting the Lord again, even in the matter of retraining his valuable herding dog.

Lauren stared up at the ceiling, unable to fall asleep for all the thoughts tumbling through her mind. Robert's large presence in her small apartment had made her feel claustrophobic. Or was it some other feeling she couldn't define? She didn't like the way her feelings for the big rancher had softened. Good thing Sam had stuck around for an hour or so to take Zoey's mind off of Lady's absence. Lauren missed the adorable dog, too.

Should she go to the local animal shelter and get another pet? Maybe a cat, an older indoor kitty that could stay home alone all day and not require twice daily walks. That might be a good Christmas present for Zoey. Besides, if they adopted a dog, it might not have Lady's protective instincts. Zoey hadn't told her about the traffic incident, and Lauren had difficulty hiding her shock. After Sam left, she'd scolded Zoey.

Zoey had just shrugged it off. *I didn't want to worry you, Mom.*

Her daughter wanted her independence, but that incident proved she wasn't ready for it yet. "Lord, please remind her to be more careful. And please protect her when she's not paying attention." The thought of losing her daughter was more than Lauren could bear. Hadn't she suffered enough loss already?

Chapter Nine

On Saturday morning, Lauren went to the mailbox just inside the building's front door. As expected, Mrs. Walston poked her head out of her apartment. "Good morning, dear." She wore her usual maternal smile. "I don't want to hold you up, but I wondered if Zoey's told you anything about theme week starting Monday and homecoming next Saturday?"

"Theme week and homecoming?" Lauren's mommy-heart dipped. Zoey had been hurt last year when a boy at her old school had pretended to ask her to the homecoming dance, then called it off the day of the dance. At least they'd been able to take the unworn dress back to the store. No wonder Zoey hadn't mentioned the upcoming event.

"Yes, indeed." Mrs. W's smile broadened. "When I was teaching, I loved these events more than all the other student activities, even prom. A theme is posted for each day, and students can wear costumes to match it. Beach Day, Pirate Day, Flower Child Day, Favorite Book Character Day…"

Lauren smiled at the dear lady's enthusiasm. "And Cowboy Day?"

"Oh, no." Mrs. W. laughed. "Most of them are cowboys all year long, so that's one theme they don't bother with." She patted Lauren's arm. "Now, I just wanted you to know that I have several costumes Zoey can borrow for the daily themes. And our church has what we call our Princess Closet to provide formal dresses for special events like homecoming and prom so parents don't have to spend money on a gown their daughter will wear only one time. We have quite a collection of closeout gowns from several bridal shops in the area, and we loan them to the girls for the school dances. No charge, of course. If Zoey would like to come down after school one day this coming week, we can find a special dress for her to wear."

"Oh, wow." Lauren's heart swelled with appreciation. "I know she'll enjoy theme week, but I don't know if she's going to the dance. If she does, a borrowed dress would be answered prayer." And before she even had a chance to pray about it.

"Good." Mrs. W. patted her hand. "A pretty girl like her should have several nice boys lining up to ask her, but sometimes the students go in groups instead of dating. One way or the other, I'm sure she'll want to attend." She turned toward her door, then back again. "Oh, by the way, the school always appreciates parent volunteers who can help out at the dance. You know, serving punch and cookies…and of course keeping an eye on the young people. At these special events, the teachers can't do it all. You may want to volunteer your services."

"Thanks. I'll do that." This woman was turning out to be a good neighbor. A little bossy, maybe, but not in a bad way like a certain other person Lauren knew.

After last year's unhappy experience, Zoey might not expect much of the homecoming dance, but if the small group of friends she'd made at school invited her, Lauren would be sure to volunteer to help so she could drive her there and keep tabs on her. But she would definitely wait for Zoey to receive an honest invitation before talking to her about a dress and the theme week costumes.

She didn't have long to wait. After church the next day, Mandy and Grace, another classmate, joined Zoey and Lauren on the church's front lawn.

"Miss Lauren, homecoming is next Saturday, and after the

football game, a bunch of us kids are going to the dance to-gether," Mandy said. "Can Zoey come with us?"

Zoey gave Lauren a pleading look. "Please, Mom." She sounded like she didn't expect her approval.

Thank You, Lord, for preparing me for this.

"Sure. That sounds like fun." She smiled at Zoey's surprised grin. "Who else is going?"

They named two other girls Lauren hadn't met yet. All the more reason for her to volunteer to help so she could see if these girls were acceptable friends for Zoey.

"Want to go for pizza with us now?" Grace asked Zoey.

"Mom?" Again, Zoey pleaded with a look.

"Well, uh…" Lauren and Zoey usually got a burger after church and talked about Pastor Tim's sermon. Was it time to let go a little bit? "Who's driving?"

"My cousin June." Mandy's hopeful expression mirrored Zoey's. "She's twenty, almost twenty-one, and a safe driver. I promise we'll bring Zoey home safely."

Lauren briefly pondered the situation. She'd met June, who taught pre-K Sunday school, and she seemed trustworthy and mature for her age. Lauren didn't want to deny her daughter this chance to have fun with friends.

"Okay." She reached into her purse, dug out her last twenty-dollar bill and handed it to Zoey. She'd have to eat a sandwich at home, but it was worth it to see Zoey have friends. Still… "Just keep your phone handy."

"Thanks, Mom." Zoey gave her a quick hug.

Her emotions mixed, Lauren watched the girls hurry across the lawn toward a blue four-door pickup, where June waited. She waved and smiled, and Lauren returned the gesture.

"It's hard to let them go, isn't it?" Andrea Mattson approached, looking sharp in her lavender pantsuit, with a floral scarf draped perfectly around her shoulders and fancy gray Western boots peeking out from beneath her trouser hemline.

"How about you joining us for lunch?" She tilted her head toward another pickup, this one an elegant burgundy red, where Linda and Andy Mattson stood. "We usually go to the steak house for Sunday lunch."

We? Did that include Robert? The pickup wasn't his black diesel monster, so maybe he had other plans. But she'd given Zoey her last twenty dollars, and she didn't dare use her one emergency credit card. "I'm not sure…"

"Come on." Andrea slipped her arm around Lauren's waist. "My treat."

Could this woman read her mind? Only pride would keep her from accepting such a kind offer, especially when she didn't really want to eat alone at home. "Sure. Thank you. I'll meet you there."

"Nonsense. Ride with us in the truck. We'll bring you back to get your car later." She tugged on Lauren's arm. "Let's go. We don't want to miss our reservation."

Did they have to make a reservation at their own restaurant? "O-okay." She let Andrea guide her across the fading lawn. To her shock, Robert also walked in that direction. How could she get out of this situation without offending Andrea?

"Hey, Lauren." He opened the front passenger door. "Here you go, Mom." He gave Andrea a hand up, then opened the back door. "Hope you don't mind sitting back here with the hired help." He nodded toward Andy and Linda as he assisted Lauren to climb in.

"Hey, watch it, Cuz." Andy sent him a phony glare, while Linda laughed.

Lauren laughed, too. Maybe this wouldn't be so bad after all. "Where's that big black truck of yours?"

He shut the door and walked around to the driver's seat. Once he'd punched the ignition start button, he spoke over his shoulder. "That's just for heavy ranch work. This is my everyday ride." Everyday ride? With its gray leather seats and a lit up computer dashboard resembling big city lights? Pretty fancy for every day.

The restaurant, located near the center of town, already had a parking lot filled with more trucks than Lauren could count. Most people around here drove them, whether they lived in town or on one of the many ranches in the area. Robert pulled into a parking spot marked Reserved. No surprise there.

Inside, they were greeted by various patrons and numerous other Mattsons, including newlyweds Will and Olivia and their two cute little children. Sam sat with friends, some of whom she recognized as clients of the law office.

"Order whatever you like. This is my favorite." Andrea pointed to a picture of a center cut ribeye on the menu.

What a gracious way to help Lauren order a juicy steak rather than search the menu for the cheapest item, as her parents had taught her to do when someone else was buying. "Thanks. I'll get it, too."

Robert and Andy sat across the table talking ranch work, while Linda and Andrea traded news about their grown children. With Linda and Andy being Sam's parents, Lauren listened politely. She'd learned in a previous job that it wasn't wise to learn too much about one's employer, but these ladies didn't seem clued in to that insight. With this being a rather tight community, she supposed everybody knew everybody else's business anyway. All she could do was pretend not to pay attention. But when their orders arrived and Robert said, "Let's pray," she had to admit knowing this was a family of faith reassured her about Zoey's involvement with their kids.

"Is Bobby slated for the starting lineup for the homecoming game?" Andy cut into his steak and took a bite.

"Not sure," Robert said. "He's big enough to mix it up with the guys, but as a sophomore, I wouldn't be surprised if Coach had somebody else in mind to start. Sad to say, we've got a pretty weak lineup this year since several of our best players graduated last year."

"Speaking of football, Lauren," Andrea said, "I heard you say Zoey has your permission to go to the homecoming dance."

Robert snorted. "Mom, only you can connect football with a dance."

The others, including Lauren, laughed.

"Humph." Andrea snatched up a dinner roll and buttered it. "It's a homecoming tradition. Do you think everybody returns home just for the game? Nonsense. They come back to watch the parade and the game, but also to socialize at the dance."

"That's so true." Lauren spoke without thinking, then took a bite of steak to keep from saying more. She really shouldn't intrude in this family conversation.

"So what event did you like best when you were in school?" Robert stared at her with those startling blue eyes. "The game or the dance?"

Heat flooded her face, and she looked down at her plate. Oh, how she hated her feminine response to his all-too-appealing good looks. "Well…"

"Did you have a brother—" he raised one eyebrow in a teasing way "—or a boyfriend who played on the football team? That's usually what draws a girl's interest to the game." He looked at Andy, who nodded and grinned his agreement.

"Surely you jest." Lauren laughed at the chauvinistic comment. "Actually, my brother was into computers, so he was on the programming team rather than playing football."

Frowning, Robert stabbed at his steak. "Huh. Just what I didn't need to hear."

How rude. "I'll have you know not one of those boys who played at our school grew up to have NFL careers or even went on to play in college." To hide her annoyance, she tried to keep her tone cheerful and teasing. "On the other hand, my brother has had a solid career as a software engineer and even coaches the programming team at the university."

After a moment of quiet, during which Robert chewed his last bite of steak, Andrea spoke up.

"Your family must be so proud." She waved to the server. "Shall we order dessert?"

Still annoyed, and a bit confused, by Robert's attitude, Lauren decided to indulge in the chocolate cheesecake on the menu. She'd worry about the calories later. Maybe run some laps around the block. Maybe never come out to Sunday dinner with the Mattsons again.

Rob learned long ago to just go along with whatever Mom planned, at least in the social realm. Count on her to invite Lauren for lunch since Mandy had taken Zoey for pizza. Everything was going fine until she had to bring up her brother's programming career. Good thing Bobby had opted to hang out with his friends rather than come to the steak house for lunch so he didn't hear her comment. Rob could only hope his son never learned about it. Rob didn't know much about Lauren's upbringing, but he doubted her parents had a business they'd spent a lifetime building so they could pass it on to their son.

Of course Lauren had no idea why her brother's success should bother him. He could tell she'd been hurt when he'd dismissed her proud declaration as something he didn't need to hear. He couldn't fix that without exposing his own pain over Bobby's disinterest in the future he should love.

Besides, why did Lauren refuse to look directly at him most of the time? A man could discern a lot about another person who never looked him straight in the eye. Was it guilt? Months before Jordyn's death, she'd started hiding something he couldn't figure out and rarely looked at him square in the eye. It wasn't until after her accident he learned what she'd been up to. By then it was too late to protect her...from herself.

Maybe the best way to solve his confusion over his unwanted attraction to Lauren would be to avoid her whenever possible. Not that Mom would understand and cooperate. She seemed to have adopted this single mother as her latest cause. Andy might be the one to help. That was it. When Zoey and Lauren came out to the ranch for Zoey's next ride, Rob would ask his cousin to oversee the lesson. That would reduce the time spent with her. Problem solved.

But if that was true, why did the plan cause an ache in his belly that had nothing to do with the salty caramel cookie he'd foolishly eaten for dessert on top of the sixteen-ounce steak and loaded potato he'd devoured? No, Rob wouldn't shirk his responsibility to make sure Zoey stayed safe when she came out to ride his horses, even if it meant he had to be around Lauren, too.

"You look so beautiful, honey." Lauren fussed with the puffy sleeves of the dusky pink tea-length formal Zoey had chosen from the Princess Closet.

"You're not so bad yourself." Zoey eyed the years-old basic black dress Lauren had dressed up with a purple scarf and the amethyst earrings she'd inherited from her grandmother.

"Thanks." Lauren refreshed her lipstick, then noticed Zoey copying her. They'd always done everything together, but one day soon, this baby bird would fly away. Best to treasure these precious mother-daughter moments while she could. "Did you enjoy the game?"

"Ugh. No." Zoey rolled her eyes. "Our guys were pitiful."

"They weren't so bad." She and Zoey had sat with Robert, Mandy, Andrea and Clementine for the nail-biter competition, with the girls cheering their lungs out and Robert calling plays from the stands. The Riverton Golden Eagles did their best to hold the line against the Española Sunrays, to no avail. The Golden Eagles' disappointment as the score mounted against them was palpable. "They tried their best. That's all any of us can do."

"Yeah." Zoey gave her the side-eye. "You know what I liked best about the game? It was before it started, when Savannah Reese rode into the stadium on her horse carrying an American flag in front of the cheerleaders and the team and all of them carrying American flags running after her. I just love to see the flags waving in the wind, especially when a rider carries it on horseback. Every year a senior girl gets to do that." She took a deep breath after her long speech.

"That *was* exciting and very inspiring. The parade was—"

Zoey faced her. "I want to do that."

"What?" Lauren held her breath.

"When I'm a senior, I want to carry the flag and ride into the stadium on Tripper in front of the team."

Lauren's eyes burned, but she wouldn't let the tears come. "Well, we have two years to work on that, don't we?" She managed a laugh. "I'm not sure good ol' Tripper would be able to gallop around the field fast enough to make the flag wave, but maybe—" She had to stop. It wouldn't do any good to encourage her daughter's dream about such a dangerous activity she'd probably never get to do.

A frown crossed Zoey's forehead. "Mom, I'm nervous about the dance. I'm glad you're going, too."

Whew. Fast change of subject. "Me too, honey. We'll have a good time."

"Uh, no. *We* won't have a good time. You just stay behind the refreshment table and serve the punch." She gave Lauren a cheeky grin. "And *I* will pretend I don't know you."

This was new and a tiny bit hurtful. The baby bird truly was getting ready to fly away. But an hour later when she took up her post behind the large glass punch bowl, she noticed it was typical of the kids whose mothers were also volunteers. It was like they were saying, *Be there for me, Mom, but I'll pretend you aren't.*

In the dimly lit gymnasium, the boys wore Western-style suits and bolo ties and the ever-present cowboy boots. Many of the girls also wore boots with their formal gowns, something that gave Lauren a chuckle. A floral archway stood at the entrance of the gymnasium, and the country-western band struck up a fanfare to announce the homecoming court. Among them were Mandy and her escort as the sophomore attendants. Years ago, Lauren had that honor as a junior at her high school, and she would much prefer Zoey to run for that office instead of aspiring to ride a horse at breakneck speed around the stadium. Across the room, she saw Robert watch his daughter with obvious pride. Surely Mandy would be chosen to carry the flag when the girls were seniors.

After the homecoming court and queen and king were introduced, the music began again, and the older students paired up and began to dance. Zoey and her friends clustered together by the folded bleachers, keeping time with the lively music and trying for all they were worth not to look at the cluster of boys, who were also trying not to look their way.

At last, Bobby broke from the herd and headed toward the girls. To Lauren's relief and joy, he held out his hand to Zoey. Lauren couldn't hear what he said, but Zoey's sweet smile spoke volumes. She and Zoey had practiced some steps at home, and it showed in the way she managed to follow Bobby's surprisingly smooth leading. Robert must have taught him.

As she watched her daughter partner with other boys in various numbers, Lauren's heart could hardly contain the joy at the way these young people accepted Zoey. For all of her worries and prayers about her daughter's future, it seemed she was on her way to a normal life. As normal as it could be.

Rob leaned back against the gym wall, arms crossed, watching the events unfold. He usually didn't mind being a prominent presence at any public gathering. It came with the territory of being a community leader and the owner of the largest cattle ranch in the area. But he'd promised Bobby and especially Mandy that he'd keep his distance so as not to embarrass them. So, after letting them out of the truck, he'd waited five minutes before going into the gym.

Then, as he'd walked down the dimly lit hallway, he could hear some male students talking around the corner.

"She's such a freak," a familiar voice said. "I'd like to see her fall flat on her ugly face." He'd spoken in a mock-halting voice, mimicking Zoey, including the slight hum that often preceded her words. "Let's go see what we can do to make that happen." His two companions had laughed.

Rob had peered around the corner. Just as he'd suspected, it was Jeff Sizemore and two of his gang. Sizemore came from a disreputable family that had caused grief in this community for well over a century and, worse, were proud of it. Jeff and his friends obviously planned to harm Zoey. No, that wasn't going to happen.

"Hey." Rob had strode toward them and grasped Jeff on the shoulder. "You cause trouble, and you'll have me to deal with."

Jeff twisted away, sneering. "You and what army?"

Rob stepped up close and personal to tower over the skinny boy of medium height. "No army needed, son. I've dealt with your sort all my life without any help."

To his satisfaction, fear flooded the boy's eyes and his friends', too. They broke away and slunk into the gym just as the music began.

Rob had followed. He'd keep an eye on them...and Zoey, to make sure they didn't trip her or embarrass her in any other way. He'd had to subdue his anger over such cruel plans because it had been time for his own daughter to make her entrance along with the rest of the homecoming court. He was proud of Mandy for being chosen to represent the sophomore class. She looked so much like her mother, who'd been homecoming queen their senior year. Would Mandy aim for that honor in two years? Or would she say it was enough to have been in the court this year? He should be proud of her willingness to let others be recognized by their peers, but it was hard for him not to want her to repeat her beautiful mother's success.

After the court had been introduced and the dance music began, Rob had found a corner to watch from, keeping his distance as he'd promised the twins.

"Hey, Rob." Rex Blake, with his sweet wife, Annie, joined him. "Looks like the kids are having a good time." As always at formal high school events, Rex wore his dress uniform to remind rowdy kids to behave themselves.

"Yep. Say, I'm glad you're here." Rob gave his good friend a brief report on what the Sizemore kid had planned.

"That's so cruel," Annie said. "From what my kids have told me, Zoey is such a sweetheart. Why would anyone want to hurt her?"

"Maybe her popularity and their lack of it makes 'em jealous." Rex shook his head. "We'll keep an eye on them *and* her. In the meantime, I'm gonna dance with my lady." He and Annie took to the floor alongside the students.

Rob hadn't planned to dance. Then he noticed Lauren serving punch at the refreshment table. As the evening wore on, he wondered if anyone would ask her out onto the floor, but no one approached her. Maybe the married male teachers and fathers of students thought partnering with the beautiful lady would cause their own lady to be jealous. He resisted as long as he could, because this fascination with a possibly devious woman was dangerous to his sense of wellbeing. Then she started rocking around keeping time with the two-step song the band struck up. Before Rob could tell his feet what to do, they did it on their own, skirting the edges of the basketball court to avoid bumping into the couples crowding the floor.

He reached the refreshment table just as Rex arrived from the other side.

"Ms. Parker, would you do me the honor—" Rex extended a hand.

Rob didn't let him finish. "Lauren, I believe this is our dance."

Looking at Rob, then Rex, she blinked, and her jaw dropped. "I...oh, here." She grabbed up the ladle, filled a disposable cup with pink lemonade from the large, glass punch bowl and thrust it across the table toward a short, brown-haired boy. "Here you go." After receiving his polite "Thank you," she stared back and forth between Rob and that pesky sheriff who used to be his friend five minutes ago. Didn't this guy still have a wife somewhere in the room?

Lauren looked awful cute in her confusion. "I'm really supposed to stay here or some of the kids might decide to spice up the punch."

Rex snorted out a laugh. "You go on and dance with that varmint." He hooked a thumb toward Rob. "I'll watch over the refreshments."

"Oh, thanks. You're so sweet." Here came that smile of hers that could knock Rob back a few feet. She sent it to Rex, then Rob.

Somehow he managed to keep his cool as he led her onto the dance floor. What was wrong with him? He'd only asked her to dance because nobody else had. In a way, he was copying Bobby, who'd set the standard by asking Zoey out to the floor. But now that Rob had his hand on Lauren's waist and his other hand holding hers, he could barely get his feet to move to the music. Finally, he forced a step, and more followed. As she had at his Labor Day celebration at the ranch, she followed smoothly, almost like she belonged here in his arms.

Whoa! This has to stop. He wasn't about to fall for her, no matter how pretty she looked as she stared up at him with that gorgeous smile. No telling what she was hiding behind it.

"I believe it's customary to have some conversation while we dance." She punctuated her statement with a laugh.

He noticed she didn't look directly into his eyes but seemed focused on his chin. With him being a head taller, maybe she didn't want to get a crick in her neck. Yeah. That was it.

"Okay." He smirked. "What do you want to talk about?"

"So you want me to start?" She laughed again, a pleasant, feminine sound. "All righty, then. How about them Golden Eagles?" Her pretty lips formed a saucy grin.

"Ugh." He winced. "You sure know how to hurt a sports fan's feelings." He shook his head. "Not to mention a father's. Coach and I are counting on Bobby growing into his natural inherited leadership abilities any day now."

"Oh, right. That's the expectation, isn't it?"

They moved around the floor for several moments before she spoke again.

"You know, kids need to find their own futures, not become what we want them to be. Zoey tells me Bobby's really good at computer programming. Maybe football's just not his thing."

Rob noticed she didn't mention ranching, and he wouldn't, either. If forced to let Bobby choose, he might be able to let football go after his son graduated, but as long as he lived, he'd never let Bobby give up his responsibility to continue the family ranching legacy.

The music ended, and he gave her a slight bow. "Thank you, ma'am." Before he could escort her back to the refreshment table, the band director announced a line dance. Rob grasped Lauren's soft hand, which had felt so good in his larger one. "Want to try line dancing again?"

"Thanks, but I should get back to my job so Sheriff Blake can dance with his wife." She nodded toward the table where Annie had joined her husband.

"Okay." He walked her across the floor and released her with another bow. "Thank you for the dance."

"Thank you." Again, she didn't look directly into his eyes. Could he really attribute that to hiding a secret? Or was it just shyness? He'd never spent time with women near his own age because Jordyn had been his one and only sweetheart since eighth grade. So he'd never learned to read all the signals women sent out. But until he knew the truth about Lady's abduction, he wouldn't be able to trust Lauren. Maybe he'd try to call that Santa Fe vet again on Monday. Or maybe he'd put it off *again* so he wouldn't have to deal with his ridiculous growing admiration for this woman.

Chapter Ten

With the words to "I Could Have Danced All Night" from her favorite musical, *My Fair Lady*, singing through her brain, Lauren could hardly sleep. What was wrong with her? While Robert Mattson might try to mold his children's lives through his cowboy version of Henry Higgins, she was no Eliza Doolittle. Hadn't she spent the last thirteen years since her divorce refusing to accept attentions from bossy men like her ex-husband?

Not that Robert had said anything controlling to her last night. In fact, she'd enjoyed the firm grip of his calloused hand in hers as he guided her around the gym floor. Had enjoyed the gentle touch of his other hand at her waist. What would it be like to be protected by such a strong, upright man? From the vantage point of her spot behind the refreshment table, she'd noticed he didn't ask anyone else to dance. Why had he singled her out?

Honestly, Lauren, you have officially lost your mind. Can't you see you're contradicting yourself? Besides, it was one dance, not a lifelong commitment. She rolled over and pulled the covers up over her ears to shut out the ticking of the wall clock above her bed. But the music in her mind refused to be quiet. She truly could have danced all night.

To her relief, she woke on Sunday morning to the words of another song Zoey was singing while she got ready for church.

The worshipful words of "Great Is Thy Faithfulness" lifted her heart and seemed to promise this would be another beautiful fall day at church. Last night, she'd accepted an invitation from another single mom to attend her Sunday school class before the main service, so they would be leaving for church an hour earlier than usual. And she always looked forward to the wisdom of Pastor Tim's sermons and the biblical truths he shared. Would Andrea ask her to lunch at the steak house again? She tried not to get her hopes up. After all, Robert's mother might want to treat someone else to lunch today.

After making sure Zoey found her own class, Lauren joined her new friend, Trudy, in the adult class, which included fifteen single parents with children of varying ages. Lauren looked around to see if Robert was here, then scolded herself when she was disappointed not to see him. The other attendees welcomed her, and the lesson was inspiring, so this might be the perfect place to make more new friends who understood the struggles of raising a child alone, especially the part about when to let go.

During the break before the main service, she joined Zoey in front of the sanctuary building.

"Do you want to sit with your friends?"

Zoey shook her head. "No. I'll sit with you." She offered a weak smile. "Don't want you to get lonely."

Lauren brushed a stray strand of hair from Zoey's cheek, a ploy for checking her temperature without annoying her. No heat emanated from her skin. "Do you feel all right?" Or had something happened in her class?

"I'm just tired from last night." Her weary voice supported her words. "It just caught up with me."

"Want to go home?"

Zoey shook her head. "Oh, no. I love Pastor Tim's sermons."

Lauren sighed. "Me too. Let's go in."

The sanctuary was filling quickly, so she found room in

the back pew. Several rows down and across the aisle, she saw Robert and his family. As though he felt her gaze, he looked back at her and smiled, and her traitorous heart skipped. *Oh, my.* She was her own worst enemy.

Halfway through the sermon, Zoey stiffened, then stared ahead blankly. Lauren grabbed her purse and dug out the midazolam nasal spray Zoey hadn't needed since last summer. But she couldn't use it until Zoey was awake.

"Excuse me," she whispered to the woman on Zoey's other side. "My daughter is ill. Please help me lay her down on the pew."

"Of course." The middle-aged woman helped Zoey lie down, even took off her own denim jacket and rolled it up to support Zoey's head. "Shall I call 9-1-1?"

"No. Not yet." Lauren forced down her rising panic and followed the procedure she'd memorized years ago after Zoey had her first seizure. Lay her on her side. Loosen her clothing. Don't put anything in her mouth. Time the seizure. If it was more than five minutes, call 9-1-1. She glanced at her watch. At times like this, five minutes felt like an eternity.

Last summer, Zoey had blanked out twice, both without the mild muscle spasms that had accompanied her childhood seizures. Each time, Lady had warned them of what was coming by crowding up to Zoey and urging her to sit. Oh, how Lauren missed that sweet dog. She chided herself for not realizing Zoey's tiredness was a warning this could happen.

Two ushers hurried over to help. In whispered tones, Lauren explained the situation. This wasn't an emergency…yet. Zoey would be fine as soon as she woke up. No need to cause an alarm or disturb the service. But the minutes were ticking by.

At last, Zoey blinked and focused on Lauren, then tried to sit up.

"Lie still, sweetie." Lauren set a hand on her upper arm to hold her in place.

"Sorry." Color rushed to Zoey's cheeks, not of illness but embarrassment.

"Shh," one of the ushers said. "No need to be sorry."

The final hymn was announced, and the congregation stood to sing. Lauren grabbed this opportunity to leave without causing a scene, which would only embarrass Zoey further. She would hold off on using the midazolam until they spoke to Zoey's doctor. "Can you bring a wheelchair?" She'd seen one outside in the vestibule.

The usher made quick work of fetching it and helped Lauren take Zoey out to the car. She buckled her in on the passenger side, then hopped into the driver's seat and hurried out of the parking lot before it became crowded with others leaving the service.

"You're going the wrong way, Mom."

"We're going to the ER."

"I'm okay now." Zoey didn't usually whine like this. "Just take me home."

Lauren reached over and patted her hand. "Sorry, honey. We need to be sure."

Zoey's deep, weary sigh assured Lauren she was doing the right thing.

"Let's invite Lauren to lunch again, Robert." Mom followed Rob from the pew. "I think she enjoyed herself with us last month."

"Sure." Rob would be glad to spend time with Lauren after last night. She'd refused a second dance with him, but he wasn't sure whether the line dance scared her off or that she didn't want to dance with him again. "I'll find her." Her reaction to his asking her to lunch would tell him what he wanted to know.

His height gave him the advantage of seeing over the heads of most other people leaving the sanctuary. To his disappointment, he couldn't locate Lauren and Zoey near the back pew. Maybe they were already outside. As he stood in line to shake hands with Pastor Tim, he heard Jake, one of the ushers, speaking to the clergyman.

"Her mother said she'd take her to the ER. Poor kid. She didn't look well at all."

Rob stepped closer. "Are you talking about Lauren Parker?"

"Yes," Jake said. "Her daughter had some sort of seizure—"

"Oh, no." Mom stood at Rob's elbow. "We should go."

"I'll go. You collect the kids and get them fed."

Mom had driven her own pickup today, so Rob didn't give her a chance to answer. Putting on his hat and clutching his Bible, he jogged from the church to his truck. Of course the entire congregation was leaving church at the same time, so traffic slowly wended its way from the parking lot and out onto the street. Rob drummed his hands on the steering wheel. His father had taught him Mattsons never used their position to push ahead of other people, but sometimes, like today, he sure did want to drive over the lawn and curb to get around this congestion.

He didn't even understand the anxiety flooding his chest. When had he decided it was his responsibility to take care of Lauren and Zoey? Did Lauren even want his help? And hadn't the pastor's sermon emphasized being still and knowing God was in control? That all things worked together for good for His children? He had to choose to trust the Lord for whatever was happening with Zoey, but it sure was hard right now.

Finally, he managed to maneuver out onto the street and head toward the hospital six blocks away. He pulled into a parking space next to Lauren's little Honda and made his way inside through the ER door.

"Hey, Mr. Mattson." The receptionist focused her attention on him. "Do you need to see the doctor?"

"Hey, Marie. I'm here to check on Zoey Parker." He removed his hat and took a step toward the ER ward.

"I'm sorry, but you can't go back there." The dark-haired thirtysomething woman gave him a stern look. "Family only, unless they invite you."

This was new. People usually made way for Rob rather than block him. "Can you find out what's happening for me?"

"I can do that." Marie made a quick trip through the swinging doors and soon returned. "You can go on back. Cubicle four."

As he made his way down the curtained ward, worry crept into his mind. What was he doing here? How would Lauren react to his intrusion? He peered around the partially open curtain.

"Hi." Questions written across her pretty face, Lauren sat beside the bed where Zoey lay.

"Hey, Mr. Mattson." Zoey looked tired but not sick. "Come on in. Is Mandy with you?"

As an unfamiliar awkwardness flooded Rob, he turned his hat in his hands. "Sorry. I should have brought her. Just wanted to see how you're doing."

Zoey sighed. "Lots better than Mom thinks I am."

Lauren patted her hand. "It never hurts to be sure."

"What happened?" Nosy question he shouldn't have asked.

"She had a mild seizure."

"Does this happen often?" More nosiness. Why couldn't he keep his mouth shut?

"This is the third one since we moved here," Lauren said. "I should have realized it was coming and taken her home after Sunday school."

"This summer, Lady warned me when I was about to go blank."

"Warned you?" Go blank? A chill swept up Rob's back and made his hair stand on end.

"Yeah. She would snuggle up next to me and make me sit down. Then she'd stay with me until it was over." She emitted a soft laugh. "I usually don't know what's happened, so she was really helpful."

Rob rocked back on his heels. Lady had likely saved this girl's life more than once, and not just when she'd pulled Zoey back from the street. He had to sort through this. What if his valuable border collie had a more important job than herding cattle? What if the dog's obvious affection for Zoey was more than the usual faithfulness the breed exhibited, but a true protective instinct to care for her because of her epilepsy and CP?

No, that couldn't be. Lady was a border collie, born and bred to herd. There were other breeds that had that instinctive nurturing gift. Maybe he could put Lauren in touch with someone who raised those dogs so she could get Zoey one of her own.

"So." Lauren stared up at him, a teasing grin on her lips. "Now that you've checked on us, don't you want to meet your family for your usual Sunday lunch? I think there's a sixteen-ounce steak calling your name."

"Uh, yeah. I should at least let them know what's happening." He grimaced. "So, what *is* happening?"

"We're waiting for the doctor. Since Zoey's not in distress, he's seeing other patients first."

Rob's first impulse was to find Doc and drag him away from whatever he was doing and bring him down here to check on Zoey right away. Instead, he said, "Can I bring you something to eat?"

Lauren traded a look with her daughter. "I think we're okay. Thanks."

"Will you call me after she sees Doc?" Rob paused. She probably wouldn't want to call him. "Or Mom. She was worried when she heard about Zoey."

Lauren blinked in that cute, surprised way of hers. "Sure. I can call Andrea."

"Right." As he'd thought, she'd prefer to call Mom. That should tell him something right there. "We'll be praying for you." Rob put his hat on and left the cubicle. In a wild moment, he stopped by Marie's desk. "If there's any problem with her bill, you send it to me."

Marie, ever the professional, didn't so much as lift an eyebrow. "Thank you, Mr. Mattson." Her dismissive tone suggested she wouldn't be sending him the bill, so he'd have to talk to Edgar Johnson, the hospital administrator, to find out if Lauren needed his help, which she'd no doubt turn down if he offered it to her directly. Edgar wouldn't be in his office on Sunday, so Rob would call him tomorrow.

Still pondering his own motives and actions regarding Lauren and Zoey, he was all the way home before he realized he'd forgotten to go to the steak house for lunch. Parking the truck in the four-car garage near the big house, he didn't see Mom's smaller pickup, so she and the kids must still be at lunch. He did see Lady scampering toward him, so he bent to ruffle her fur behind her ears, only to see her look beyond him toward the truck.

"Sorry, girl. The kids aren't with me right now. They'll be home soon."

Rob waved to Grady, who sat reading a book in front of the bunkhouse, with Scotch and Irish resting on the ground beside him. One of six year-round ranch hands who lived here, Grady was taking his turn to stay home and guard the place. Even before Lady was stolen, it had been a hard, fast rule that one of the hands or a family member would take turns staying home from church to guard against thieves. The practice went all the way back to the days of cattle rustlers in the late 1800s. Before Lady's theft, nobody worried too much that anyone would actually try to steal anything from the ranch. Now everybody here, family or employee, had to be constantly vigilant.

He headed toward the house, and Lady followed him, then lay down on the back porch and watched toward the road.

"Hey, how about a little attention for me? Who do you think pays for your food?"

She gave him a brief glance before turning back to her vigil. She didn't even follow him inside for a treat. Just like Lauren, she wasn't interested in his company. Only in Lady's case, he was in charge, and he was determined to change her mind about her old job. Maybe it was time for him to take both Lady and Bobby in hand and mold them to fit the jobs they were born to do.

What had Lauren said last night? Kids need to find their own futures? But didn't they need guidance toward that future? Didn't they need to have a goal and a coach to push them toward it?

As more memories from last night came to mind, he took some leftover meatloaf from the fridge and didn't bother to heat it in the microwave before taking a bite. Ugh. Should have gone back to the restaurant for steak.

Last night, he couldn't have been prouder of Bobby for asking Zoey to dance. Like all the Mattson men before him, Bobby was a gentleman who did right by his friends. And both he and Mandy had that built-in radar to warn them about kids who tried to get close to them because of their family's place in the community. Zoey wasn't one of those. That was why he encouraged the twins' friendship with her. She had a sweet innocence about her and seemed more concerned about what other people needed rather than using her disability to her advantage. His kids could enjoy her company without worries about being used. Then there was the way she helped them both with their homework. Although they'd only known her for less than two months, she already seemed like an honorary member of the family. He enjoyed interacting with her, and she was friendly to him in return...unlike Lauren, who kept him guessing about her opinion of him.

That was probably best, at least for him. Lauren could have latched on to him like a couple of local women had tried to do after Jordyn died. Instead, she refused his offers of help and didn't seem interested in spending time with him. She'd been reluctant to dance with him last night and refused a second one. Of course she had let him pay for last week's lunch at the steak house. No, she'd accepted it because Mom had invited her. And he had yet to meet anybody who could resist Mom's hospitality.

None of this pointed to a woman who would steal a valuable dog. So why didn't he just try again to reach that vet and get Lauren's story confirmed? Easy answer. Because he just couldn't stand the idea that he might learn she'd been a part of Lady's dognapping.

Lauren settled Zoey in her bed, grateful that the doctor had found nothing serious when he examined her. This episode had been similar to those she had this past summer. Doc's main concerns were that Zoey had become dehydrated and that she'd probably eaten too much sugar at last night's dance, thus bringing on this morning's seizure. He did give her clearance to resume her riding lessons, as long as she kept hydrated and took her anticonvulsant medication.

She heated a can of chicken noodle soup and took it to Zoey's room, only to find her sound asleep. And no wonder. These episodes always wore her out. Lauren returned to the kitchen and ate the soup.

She didn't know what to make of Robert showing up at the hospital. Which reminded her, she'd promised to call Andrea. She grabbed her phone and punched the first number under Andrea's name. Surely by now her friend would be home from lunch.

"Double Bar M Ranch." Robert's baritone voice boomed into her ear.

For a few beats, Lauren couldn't speak for the strangely pleasant shiver that swept down her back.

"Um, Robert?" *Duh!* Of course it was Robert. *Oh, no.* She must have called the ranch's landline when she should have called Andrea's cell phone.

He chuckled, sending another shiver down her neck. "Yeah. Hey, Lauren." Pause. "How's Zoey?"

"She's sleeping." Lauren took a breath. "I meant to call your mother. Sorry for the—"

"Don't be sorry." She could hear the smile in his voice. "I'm glad you called here. What did Doc say?"

Lauren gave him a brief report.

"So, does that mean she can come back out to the ranch next Saturday and resume her riding lessons?"

At the borderline eagerness in his tone, Lauren couldn't speak for a moment. "Yes, that would be nice. In fact, he said it would be good exercise as long as she takes her meds and stays hydrated. Do you mind?"

He chuckled. "Not at all. The kids always enjoy having her out here." Pause. "We all do."

Her heart warmed. "Oh. Okay. Thanks. We'll come. Guess that means I'll have to do my laundry on Friday night." Had she actually said that out loud? What was wrong with her?

Robert laughed. "You do that."

"Okay," she repeated. "See you Saturday."

"Good." He didn't hang up, but seemed about to say more.

"Did you have something else to say?"

"You called me, remember?" Another deep, shiver-inducing chuckle. "Did *you* have something else to say?"

At his repetition of her words, Lauren punched the mute icon on her phone and giggled like a schoolgirl. This was so silly. So…so…she didn't know what. She took a deep breath before punching the icon again. "Zoey wants some boots for when she rides. Do you know where I can get a pair for a reasonable price?" Oh, no. That sounded like she was asking for charity.

"Better than that. We probably have a pair around here that'll fit her."

Lauren sighed. Oh, how she longed for her daughter to have more than she could provide. This family had already given her and Zoey so much, but only pride would make her refuse. "Thanks." Then she could see if Zoey could actually wear Western boots without spending any money for a new pair.

"Say," Robert said, "what would you think about joining me for that new Bible study Pastor Tim announced today? It starts a week from this Wednesday. Don't know about you, but I'm interested in what that Hebrew scholar has to say about Genesis."

Was he asking her out? Or just offering a ride to church? Either way, this was her first such invitation in all the years since Singleton had divorced her in favor of a perfect...and *pregnant* younger woman, so he could have a perfect child. Not many men wanted to spend time with a woman once they found out she had a child with a disability.

Silly tears burned her eyes. She swallowed hard to keep the emotion from her voice. "I'd like to hear him, too." She'd have to ask Mrs. W. to spend that evening with Zoey or at least check in on her. "Yes, I'll join you."

"Great." He hesitated. "Maybe we could have a bite to eat beforehand?" The up tone at the end of his sentence made it a question instead of his usual bossiness. It also made him sound a little uncertain.

Bless his heart, he was nervous! She should meet him halfway. "Sounds good." More than good. Nothing short of exciting.

But after they ended the call, she slumped back in her chair in horror. What had she just done? Yes, she was interested in the Genesis study, but going with Robert might send the wrong signals to…well, to somebody…to *everybody*.

"Mom?" Zoey came into the room rubbing her eyes. "I heard you laughing. What's up?"

Lauren stood and embraced her. "Hungry?" She'd always shared everything with Zoey, but now she had to sort out her conversation with Robert before telling her about it. In truth, she could already see the obvious. Her association with him had just turned a big corner. Whether it would lead to something good or to another heartbreak, only time would tell.

Chapter Eleven

Rob scratched his head in confusion. What had he just done? He'd never once thought about asking any woman, much less Lauren Parker, to go anyplace with him. Of course, this was a church Bible study, but from her subdued response, she wasn't exactly thrilled. Maybe she'd change her mind, and he wouldn't have to follow through. If he could have seen her face, it would have told him what he needed to know. In the meantime, how was he going to explain it to his kids? To Mom? Not that she hadn't already been silently pushing him toward Lauren since the first time she and Zoey visited the ranch. She'd be as happy as a trout biting on a May fly to know he'd asked the woman to go with him somewhere, but especially to Bible study.

Maybe it wasn't all bad. Getting closer to her should reveal the truth of her character. And he still had this coming Saturday to spend in her company. To say he couldn't wait for the week to pass didn't fully explain his eagerness.

With regular ranch work to oversee, including making sure his prize bull, Buster, was doing his duty by the cows, checking through the hay storage barn to be sure it held enough for winter, not to mention his responsibilities to the Riverton Cattlemen's Association, Rob had plenty to keep him busy. But in the back of his mind, and sometimes right up-front, interfering with what he was doing at the moment, he couldn't get Lauren off his mind. She was beautiful, kind and thoughtful. And fun, at least when she was with the kids. Of course he'd prefer that she responded to him a little more openly, but that was probably shyness on her part. He didn't know much about her ex-husband, only that Sam had told him the man had remarried. How could he have let her and Zoey go? Rob had no idea how big-city folks regarded marriage, but he'd always believed it to be sacred, a commitment not only to his wife, but to the Lord. How did a man justify breaking his marriage vows?

Saturday arrived, bringing Lauren and Zoey to the ranch at midmorning. Remembering his promise to provide boots for Zoey, Rob had dug out several pairs of Jordyn's old ones that didn't fit Mandy. Only after he brought several pairs downstairs did he realize he no longer felt the sharp pain in his heart that usually accompanied anything to do with Jordyn's belongings. It wasn't that he didn't still love her, still miss her, but she would be happy to see her boots going to a deserving girl.

He saw them arrive through the back window. Mandy and Bobby ran out to meet them, with Lady racing ahead to greet Zoey. The way that dog wagged herself silly around Zoey made her preference clear, and the girl obviously loved her in return.

Maybe... No, he had to shut down that train of thought. Lady belonged to Bobby, and that was that. Once football season was over, maybe even before, Rob would work with them before and after school every day to train them both for the jobs they were born to do.

He stepped out on the back porch and waved. "Mornin'. Had your coffee yet?"

Lauren walked through the gate. "Yes, but I can always drink another cup."

Her smile hit him right in the chest. Wow, she was beautiful. "Great. Come on in. You too, Zoey. I have some boots for you to try on."

"For me? Really?" She gave him a big grin.

Once they were inside and Mom had served coffee to Lauren, with the kids opting for sodas, Zoey tried on the boots, finally settling on a weathered tan-and-brown pair. "These feel good. Thanks."

Rob noticed Lauren's sneakers. "How about you? Want to try these on?" He held up a red, white and blue pair Jordyn had never gotten around to wearing.

"Oh, I don't know."

"It won't hurt to try them on." He pushed them toward her, and before she got the wrong idea, he added, "They're lots better than sneakers for walking around the barn and corral."

"Oh. Okay. Thanks." Again, her beautiful smile stirred up that pesky tickle in his chest.

She sat on a kitchen chair and pulled off a sneaker, then stuck her foot into one of the boots. And took it off with a laugh. "Well, it's a bit big. I'd need some mighty thick socks to be able to wear them. Just call me Footloose. Or Bootloose. Or something like that."

Rob laughed, as did Mom and the kids. It felt good, like they were all one family.

No, that was *not* what he meant. Or was it?

Lauren liked to hear Robert laugh. It was a melodious baritone chuckle that emanated from deep inside him and made her smile. He was proving not to be the grouchy old bear she and Zoey had met less than two months ago. Apparently he'd forgotten their introduction came about when he'd accused her of stealing Lady. That was a relief.

While driving out here, she'd felt some moments of trepidation before remembering the day wasn't about her, but Zoey. What little girl didn't want to ride horses? Lauren sure had. But even with numerous horse farms in Central Florida, she'd never had the opportunity to visit them or even climb into a saddle. Now her daughter had a chance to ride. And maybe one day she could, too, if she could drum up enough courage to try. Daydream pictures of taking lessons from Robert came to mind, but she quickly dismissed them as flights of fancy.

In the barn, Zoey did her share of stall mucking before helping Mandy put a bridle and saddle on Tripper. The old gelding had perked up the minute they approached his stall, as though he was as eager for a ride as the kids were. Lady greeted Tripper, meeting him nose to nose in a friendly gesture. And, as before, Robert leaned against the wall, arms crossed and watched, which Lauren appreciated. Bobby and especially Mandy were clearly competent in caring for Tripper, but it was good for their dad to be available. From the pleasant look on his handsome face—yes, she admitted to herself again, he was handsome—he enjoyed this as much as the kids. Which revealed his generous heart as much as letting Zoey wear his late wife's boots. And being concerned about her own footwear, even though the pair he offered hadn't fit her.

"By the way." Robert moved closer to Lauren and spoke in a low voice close to her ear. "The Bible study this week starts at eight at the fellowship hall. Can I pick you up for supper around six?"

As before, a pleasant shiver swept down her side. This time she didn't try to stop it. "Sure. That works for me." Did she sound breathless?

Lady was as involved in the morning's riding lesson as the kids. She sat at the ready just inside the corral fence, her eyes on Zoey's every movement as she rode Tripper. When Zoey tipped to the side, Lady stood and took a step toward the horse. But with Bobby and Mandy walking on either side of Tripper, Zoey soon regained her balance, so Lady settled back down.

Watching from outside the fence, Lauren resisted mentioning to Robert the way Lady focused her protective attention on Zoey. His attention was focused on the kids, which she appreciated. To think that this busy rancher took time to be concerned about her daughter should be enough. Yet it would give her so much relief if Zoey could have Lady with her all the time, especially when Lauren couldn't be with her.

The morning went by all too fast. Once again, Andrea insisted Lauren and Zoey must stay for lunch. Her tuna salad had a delicious flavor Lauren hadn't been able to replicate even when following Andrea's recipe.

"Lauren," Andrea said from her end of the table. "I hope you'll sit with us in church tomorrow."

Zoey and Mandy put their heads together and whispered something, then giggled. Lined up with Clementine on the other side of the table, the girls looked like mischief waiting to happen.

Lauren studiously avoided turning toward Robert, who sat at the other end of the table. "Thanks. We'll see how the morning goes."

In truth, she preferred to sit at the back in case Zoey had another episode. If she did and they were seated in the middle of the sanctuary, they would interrupt the service and embarrass both of them.

She needn't have worried. Zoey took her meds and kept hydrated. On Sunday morning, she eagerly met up with Mandy. Seeing her daughter have such a good friend at last was an answered prayer, but what were these two girls up to? Was it just chatter about boys? Probably.

Invited to after-church lunch again, Lauren found herself seated next to Robert due to Andrea's maneuvering, with Linda and Andy making up the rest of the party. Robert's pleasant spicy aftershave only added to his manly presence, and she had to still the fluttering in her heart. This was ridiculous. She had no intention of falling for this man, no matter how kind he was to her and Zoey.

After they'd put in their order, he leaned close and whispered, "I think our girls are up to something. What do you think?"

As she tried without success to quell the pleasant shivers going down her arm, she looked across the restaurant dining room where the girls sat with Bobby and some other kids.

"Oh, probably just the usual teenage chatter." She smiled up at Robert. At his intense, blue-eyed gaze, she had to look away. He was the classic ruggedly handsome cowboy. The kind who rode in and saved the day, then, like a true gentleman, tipped his hat to his leading lady before riding off into the sunset. She'd fallen for a perfectly handsome, well-mannered man once before and had her heart broken. If only she could tell that heart to be more careful with this one, but she didn't seem to have control over it at the moment.

She cleared her throat. "You know how kids like to dramatize everything."

He chuckled in his warm, deep-voice way, and her heart took another dip. "I've noticed that."

"What are you two whispering about?" Linda gave Robert a little smirk. "Let's not have any secrets."

He shrugged. "Just talking about how to raise our kids. Y'all did a fine job with your two. Maybe you have some advice for us single parents as we navigate these teen years."

"Oh, now, let's don't go there." Andy shook his head. "You know the trouble we had with Sam as a teen. He was a handful—"

"Hey, wait a minute," Lauren interrupted. "Better not speak ill of my boss. You don't want me to lose respect for him. That would undermine his authority with me." There she went, speaking up when she should have kept quiet.

The others laughed, so she persuaded herself to relax.

"I admire your loyalty, Lauren." Robert's baritone voice once again stirred her emotions. "And your discretion. I'm sure my young cousins are glad they hired you."

The server arrived with their dinners, and Robert offered

grace before they all dug in. Lauren stirred the toppings into her loaded baked potato and took a bite.

"Most of us cattle folk start with our steak." Robert took a bite of his, as if to prove his point. "Yours okay?"

"I'll let you know." Lauren followed suit. "Mm. Delicious."

"On another topic," Linda said to Andrea, "how's your condo coming down in Phoenix?"

Lauren glanced at Robert, who frowned and stabbed into his steak a little more forcefully, his disapproval of his mother's upcoming move apparent.

"It was close to being finished, but hit a snag." Andrea responded to Linda, but gave her son a sympathetic smile. "James says he had to send back the—"

"James?" Robert almost growled the name. "Who on earth is James?" He might have been interrogating one of his kids rather than his mother.

Andrea sat up straighter and glared at him. "He's my contractor." She paused and took a breath. "And I'll warn you, I've invited him up for Thanksgiving so you can meet him."

Even without knowing this family for very long, Lauren could see Andrea's announcement made clear she had special feelings for the man who was completing her future home.

"You have, have you? Thanks for letting me know." Robert's gruff tone revealed his reaction to his mother's possible romance.

The conversation moved on to other things, but Robert's earlier compliment about Will and Sam being glad they hired her stayed with Lauren and still had the power to lift her heart when he picked her up on Wednesday evening. As always, he looked sharp in his black Western-cut blazer, blue shirt, bolo tie and classic black Stetson hat. He could definitely be a movie star.

"What sounds good?" he asked as he helped her climb up into his red pickup.

She adjusted her denim skirt on the leather seat. "I assumed we'd go to your steak house."

He chuckled, that warm sound she had come to like all too much. "Let's try something different."

"Sure."

He drove them to a cute little old-fashioned diner several blocks from the church, where the aroma of grilled onions dominated the room, country music played softly in the background and six or so other patrons occupied the tables. He greeted the middle-aged waitress like an old friend, and after she gave Lauren a quick once-over, she sat them in a back corner.

"It's nice and quiet in here." Robert took off his hat and set it on the seat beside him. "Makes it easier to have a conversation."

Uh-oh. Lauren's stomach turned, and not just because she was hungry. What did he want to talk about?

After they ordered, he settled his vivid blue gaze on her and smiled. "You know, we haven't had much of a chance to really get acquainted. I'd like to hear your story. What brought you to Riverton? Other than working for my rascally young cousins, I mean."

She blinked and stared down at the paper placemat in front of her, which advertised the diner's specialty milkshakes. Why did this suddenly feel like a job interview? Or some sort of interrogation? All of her former confidence that he had forgotten the unpleasantness of their first meeting fled. But she had nothing to hide. Might as well spill it all and be done with it.

"My story?" Lauren widened her eyes, which looked turquoise tonight, matching the pretty button-up blouse she wore. "If you want to know why I came out here, I should start with what I left behind." Her expression became guarded, and she shrugged. "It's not pretty."

Rob hadn't meant to put her on the defensive. Just wanted to know more about her and what made her tick besides raising her remarkable daughter. "Hey, we all have stuff in our pasts." He chuckled apologetically. "Didn't mean to intrude."

She gave him a half smile. "That's okay." Another shrug. "As you know, I'm divorced. Not because I wanted to be, but because my ex…" She chewed her lip. "It's always easy to make him sound like the bad guy, but—"

"But he was?" Rob grinned.

"Well…in my view, he was." She sighed. "The split was his choice. He already had a pregnant girlfriend waiting in the wings and married pretty quickly after the papers were signed."

A protective feeling stirred in his chest. "Did you have any custody problems?"

"No." Her voice sounded weary, making him sorry he'd started this. "He wasn't interested in raising a child with a disability."

What a rotten man. Rob tamped down his flash of anger. "He doesn't know what he's missing. Zoey's one terrific kid."

"Yes, she is. Thank you for seeing that. But I'm sure he's happy with his trophy wife and their two perfect kids. I rarely think about him anymore." She smiled at the waitress, who'd just set down her plate. "Thanks."

After they'd prayed for their dinner, she resumed her story between bites. "Singleton is a—"

"Singleton?" Rob snorted. "What kind of name is that?"

She laughed, a real laugh, accompanied by a twinkle in her eyes that hinted she might agree it was a ridiculous name. "Singleton Weatherby Parker. It's a family name. He's been the main news anchor at the NBC affiliate in Orlando for about fifteen years. He has an image to maintain, so having a child with a disability didn't line up with that." She huffed out a breath. "Anyway, after years of running in place in my hometown, I needed to try something new. So I applied to Mattson and Mattson online, and was so grateful that your cousins were willing to hire me even though I'd just earned my paralegal license." She gave him a cute little grin. "And just to let you know, I happen to think your 'rascally' cousins are pretty terrific young men."

He chuckled. "Yeah. It runs in the family."

"Along with a skosh of pride, at least in some of you?"

"Goes with the territory of being terrific."

Her second bout of genuine laughter dispelled his concerns that he'd made a mistake to ask about her past. It was good to know how badly she'd been treated and yet managed to survive and be an exceptional mother.

As for that Singleton Weatherby Parker—he couldn't quite get past that pretentious name—from what Rob had seen in his forty-two years, men like him were more concerned about their own wants and needs rather than taking care of the families the Lord had given them. How could any real man so easily divorce a wife he'd promised to love, honor and cherish? How could he ignore his precious child and go off to make a new family even before the divorce?

"So, what about you? What's your story?" Lauren asked before popping a bite of broccoli in her mouth.

Again, he was sorry to have opened the topic. But fair was fair.

"It's kinda boring. Raised on the ranch, took over management when my dad wanted to retire." A soft pang hit his chest. "I wouldn't say this to Mom, but I don't think he should have retired. He just didn't know what to do with himself. After sitting around twiddling his thumbs for more than a year, he died a little over two years ago."

"I'm so sorry." The sweet sympathy in her eyes made her even more beautiful. "And to lose your wife, too. That's so sad. It must have been hard for you and the kids."

"Yeah." Again, fair was fair. "She had a riding accident four years ago and broke her neck." He coughed to keep from groaning at the memory. "The fall also caused a brain bleed the doctors didn't find in time."

"Oh, how awful." Now her eyes reddened. "She was a rodeo queen, right? A good rider?"

"Being a good rider, even the best, can't save you from a horse that doesn't want to be tamed." Rob didn't want to say more, especially since Jordyn had kept her attempts to train Rowdy a secret after he'd forbidden her to work with the horse. "On that topic…" He forced a cheerful tone into his voice. "You don't have to worry about Tripper. He's a good ol' horse and hasn't ever thrown anybody. He's extra careful with kids and inexperienced riders. Just seems to have that instinct."

"Just like…" She looked down at her plate and bit her lip.

"Go on. You mean just like Lady." He should have figured they'd come around to talking about his dog.

"Yes." She looked up, and her beautiful eyes pierced him. "How's her training, uh, *re*training going?"

Rob took a bite of his Reuben sandwich to keep from answering right away. At last he said, "Not so good."

"I'm sorry. We didn't—" She stopped. "I'll pray she finds her calling again."

He stared into her eyes, loving the way they caught the light and the color of her blouse. "Thanks. I appreciate that."

How could that Singleton dude have let this woman go? Rob never would have abandoned Jordyn, even if he'd found out about her foolish attempts to train an untrainable horse. Marriage was until "death do us part." Somehow they would have worked things out.

As if to support his thoughts on the subject, the Hebrew scholar who presented the first lesson on the book of Genesis spoke at length about God's creation of man and woman and how He had given them to each other in a beautiful garden.

In particular, Rob was moved by the teacher's explanation of God's interaction with Adam. When God called to Adam, he responded, "Here I am." The Hebrew word conveyed more than physical presence. It was an awareness of Adam's deeply spiritual communion with his Creator.

To think of being in the physical presence of God and then to succumb to temptation and break that connection seemed the very definition of sin and depravity. And stupidity. Adam not only broke his relationship with God, but he didn't do right by his wife, blaming her for his failure in leadership.

The man spoke simply, quietly, but his words held his audience's attention. Rob glanced at Lauren to note her reaction, glad to see her soft, receptive expression. Maybe they could talk about the lesson later. For now, he was reminded of how many times marriage had come to mind in the past few days, weeks. And always when he was around her.

So what made a good marriage? His relationship with Jordyn had always been open and honest from the beginning when they were in middle school. He didn't know when or why or how their communication broke down. He only knew she'd started keeping secrets from him. That it was about her determination to train Rowdy and his forbidding her to do so only came to light after her tragic fall and death.

As he had many times since she died, he wondered what he would do differently if only he could go back and fix it. Adam probably thought that more than once in the years after he and Eve were thrown out of the Garden of Eden. In Rob's case, maybe he'd been too heavy-handed with Jordyn, while Adam had been too willing to, as Pastor Tim often said, *go along to get along.* Either way it didn't lead to a good marriage.

By the time Sunday rolled around again, Rob admitted to himself that spending time in Lauren's company was becoming a habit, and a good one at that. Before the Sunday evening service, he and Lauren settled in the gym bleachers next to each other while the kids played their games and burned off some energy. The twins joined in the volleyball game, and Zoey played foosball with another student. Her coordination appeared to be improving because she held her own against the boy.

"Has Bobby mentioned the computer programming event at the University of New Mexico next month?" Lauren sipped coffee from a Styrofoam cup.

Rob ground his teeth. "Yeah."

Lauren watched him for a moment. "What do you think?"

"He has a football game that Friday night, so that takes priority."

She stared at him for a moment, then shook her head and looked away.

"What?" He didn't want to ask, but did anyway.

"Oh, nothing." She gave him a little smile. "Zoey signed up for it." She sipped her coffee again. "If Bobby signs up, we could ride-share. It would make it more fun for her." Pause. "Plus making it easier for her in a new and unfamiliar situation."

"Maybe Mandy could go." Rob waved a dismissive hand. "Bobby needs to be with his team."

"As a benchwarmer? Like at the homecoming game?"

"What? No. He'll get to play." He wasn't being honest. Coach always put his seniors and juniors on the first string. Sophomores only went in when the Golden Eagles were winning by plenty of points. "Even a few minutes on the field is good training."

"But if he goes with the computer team, he'll be first string." Her cute grin held a hint of teasing.

He returned a smirk. "Right. Listen, Lauren, I know you're proud of your brother's computer programming job, but Bobby doesn't need that. His future is on the ranch. After he graduates from high school, he'll get his degree in agriculture and animal husbandry, then come back to work in the family business. He doesn't need to waste time on the intricacies of software programming."

"Seems like you have it all planned out. What does Bobby think?"

He didn't answer for a moment. "He'll come around when the time comes."

"Hmm."

Rob ignored her smug look. Maybe she just didn't understand family legacy, how each generation needed to respect and follow the path their ancestors set before them. Maybe if he took her on a tour of the ranch next Saturday and explained that history, she'd jump on board and help him encourage Bobby to quit fighting the path he was supposed to follow.

Chapter Twelve

"It's so beautiful." Lauren gazed down the hill toward the Rio Grande. "That natural earthen levee is a lot prettier than the concrete levee where the river runs through town." She couldn't guess why Robert offered this tour of his ranch, but she was enjoying every minute of it, especially when he talked about his family's history. "I guess it protects the lower fields from flooding, right?" The levee, maybe fifteen feet high and overgrown with grass and trees, stood as a barrier next to the lower pasture where around thirty cattle grazed.

Robert chuckled. "First of all, it's not natural. My ancestors build it by hand, one shovelful at a time." He grunted, as though considering that laborious task. "It took several years to finish, and each year, floods would wash away part of the previous year's work. So they had to rebuild before they could add on."

"Oh, my." She inhaled a deep breath of the cool autumn air, along with the usual smells of cattle that she was somehow getting used to. "I can't imagine all that work by hand."

"Right. Today we'd just use the backhoe and have the whole thing repaired in a matter of days. Maybe hours." He took a step down the hill, and she followed. "A man had to be pretty tough and strong in those days."

"A woman, too. Your mom's told me about some of the women who helped settle this land. Oops!" She stumbled over a hidden rock and grabbed his arm to keep from falling.

He gripped her hand and helped her regain her balance. "You okay?" The concern in his gaze sent a silly tickle through her heart.

Heat rushed to her face. "Sorry."

"No problem." He smiled, revealing his dimple. Another tickle spiked in her chest. "Even after a hundred and forty years, we still have lots of fieldstone working its way to the surface. We have to be careful riding the horses out here so they don't break a leg."

He hadn't released his gentle grip on her arm and continued to gaze down at her in his intense way. Somehow she managed not to look away, as she usually did. Maybe she was getting used to having this gorgeous cowboy stare at her like he thought she was special.

No, she must not think that way. He was only being hospitable. The twins had given Zoey her riding lesson, and after another of Andrea's delicious lunches, she was helping them with their homework. So Robert had invited Lauren for a tour of the ranch. How could she turn him down? She loved the history of this area. Loved learning about the women whose portraits hung in the hallways and great room in what they all called "the Big House." Loved hearing about his ancestors' struggles and their successes.

When he continued to hold her arm, continued to stare at her without saying anything, something inside her shifted. What did he want? What did *she* want?

He took a breath, as though about to speak, and her heart hitched up another notch.

"Daddy! Miss Lauren!" Clementine came running down the hill, waving a piece of paper.

Robert exhaled a long breath and shook his head. "What is it, Clementine?"

Lauren couldn't blame him for the hint of annoyance in his

voice. Whatever he'd planned to say was lost, perhaps forever. Still, she managed to turn a bright smile toward the little girl.

"What do you have there, sweetheart?" Lauren reached out a hand and pulled Clementine into a side hug.

"It's a picture." The child proudly thrust the page at her. "I drew it for you, Miss Lauren."

"Oh, my." Lauren wished she could hide the picture from Robert, but he was looking over her shoulder at his daughter's artwork. It depicted surprisingly good representations of their family members, plus two. Andrea, easy to spot with her graying hair, the twins, Clementine, Robert. And Zoey. And Lauren. And Lady. "Oh, my" was right. What would Robert think about this? "It's just lovely. You're an artist, sweetie. I'll take it home and put it on my fridge."

Clementine looked up at Robert. "Do you like it, Daddy?" Hunger for his praise beamed from her blue eyes. "Do you like it?"

As he often did, he patted her head, almost absentmindedly. "Sure, honey. Nice job. Now you run along. Miss Lauren and I were—"

"Miss Lauren is about to collect her daughter and go home." Lauren gave him a teasing smirk. "Laundry."

He snorted out a rueful laugh, his disappointment clear. "You and your laundry. Okay, let's go back to the house."

As they trudged up the hill, with Clementine clinging to Robert's hand, Lauren felt a different kind of tug in her heart. This darling little girl was so desperate for her daddy's attention. Didn't he realize she needed as much love and care as his older children? It might not be Lauren's place to tell him, but she could pray he would see it for himself without something drastic happening.

After rethinking Clementine's ill-timed interruption to his conversation with Lauren, Rob decided it was for the best.

He had no idea what he'd intended to say to this woman who was becoming all too important to him. Did his youngest daughter's picture foreshadow a future blended family? No, he couldn't say that yet, couldn't even say he loved Lauren. He'd have to think about it. One thing he knew. He liked her more and more every time they were together. Just as he'd hoped, she ate up the stories about his family's history. Had spoken with admiration for the pictures of the strong, tough men...and women, of course...who'd laid the foundation for this ranch and made it a success. Whether it helped Lauren understand why Bobby needed to follow in their footsteps, Rob couldn't say. But her interest, untinged by the covetousness he'd seen in other women, was open and encouraging. Or maybe she simply loved history. He'd have to spend more time with her to find out.

He and the kids walked her and Zoey to their car, with Lady sticking close to Zoey like she expected to go with her.

"No, Lady." Bobby held on to his dog's collar as she tried to climb into the little Honda. "Stay."

She struggled against his grasp until Lauren nudged Zoey's arm. "Tell her to stay."

Zoey held up a hand. "Stay, Lady."

Instantly, Lady sat on the ground by Bobby. But when the car drove out through the front gate, Lady trotted after it for a few yards until the electric gate clanged shut. Then she lay there looking like she'd lost her best friend. Only time would fix that, time in Bobby's company and with his training.

As he watched Lauren drive her little car beyond the front gate, another thought came to mind. Maybe he could have suggested they should see where their friendship was going. No, that sounded too much like teenagers in the throes of their first crush. Maybe without addressing the subject, he could simply come up with more excuses to spend time with her.

Yeah, that was it. He always had some errand or another in

town. It would be easy to drop by the law office and ask her to lunch. Or make some excuse to chat with his cousins and include her in the conversation.

In the meantime, he'd see her at church tomorrow. For some reason, she usually preferred to sit at the back, but maybe he could enlist Mandy to get Zoey to sit farther down in the middle pew where Rob's family had sat for a hundred years. Then he'd ask Mom to invite them to lunch again. He doubted she'd turn down another steak dinner.

With those plans in mind, the next morning he took special care to look his best as he got ready for church. The aromas of bacon and waffles reached him as he came down the stairs. But the scene he expected of his family seated around the breakfast table wasn't what he saw. Mom was huddled with the twins beside the stove, and they turned as one when he entered the room.

"What's going on—"

"I'm so sorry, Dad." Bobby looked like he'd been crying. "Lady's missing."

Rob's old doubts slammed into his brain, but he quickly dismissed them. How foolish to think Lauren had anything to do with this. After all, she'd reminded Zoey to tell Lady to stay. He really needed to reach that Santa Fe vet, but his second attempt the other day had been met with an outgoing voicemail message that the clinic was closed for vacation. Maybe the Lord didn't want him to reach the man.

Mom and the twins were staring at him, bringing him back to the present.

"Okay, let's eat breakfast. Lady's probably just hanging out with Scotch and Irish by the barn." He pulled out his chair and sat down. "Come on. We don't want to be late for church." He reached out a hand to Mandy, who sat on his left beside Clementine. "Let's pray. Lord, You know where Lady is and You know how much we love her. Please bring her back so she can fulfill the purpose You've given her. Amen."

Mom cleared her throat.

Rob winced. "And, Lord, thank You for Your bountiful provision for this family. May we always be mindful of all You've given us."

While he ate Mom's delicious waffles covered with butter and maple syrup, he considered staying home from church and searching every inch of the ranch. Surely Lady was hiding in some corner of the barn. Maybe she was in the lower pasture with the yearling steers practicing her herding. Yeah, no. That was unlikely.

After breakfast, he told Grady to pass the word among the ranch hands to keep an eye out for Lady, then drove the family toward town.

Halfway along the five-mile drive, he saw Lauren's unmistakable little Honda driving toward them. She must have recognized his truck from a distance because she came to a stop on the side of the road, as he did.

She rolled down her window. "Hey, cowboy. Did you lose something?"

Seated on the passenger side with Lady in her lap, Zoey grinned and waved.

If a heart could burst with happiness, Rob's would do so right now. While Mom and his three kids exclaimed their joy over seeing Lady, he hid his excitement and relief with a laugh. His suspicions about Lauren were definitely unfounded. Exiting the truck, he crossed the highway and bent down to speak to her through her open window.

"Thanks for bringing her back, Lauren. Don't know what I'm gonna do with that little gal." He could see her guarded expression. After his unfair accusations when they met, he didn't blame her. "Where did you find her?"

Lauren stepped out of her car. "We found her curled up outside our apartment building door when we came out to leave for Sunday school. Want to take her now? Or I can leave her at the ranch."

A quick consultation with Mom gave him a better plan. "We'll take her. Can you fit the kids in your car? Don't want them to be late to Sunday school."

"Sure."

The shuffle of bodies on the side of the road was more chaotic than it should have been, with each of his kids insisting on welcoming Lady back to the family, and Lady trying to wriggle free and get back to Zoey. In the truck, Mom finally had Lady in hand, more or less, so Rob shut the door to keep her from jumping out, then crossed the road again to make sure Lauren could manage the kids. Bobby had folded his lanky frame into the back seat of the Honda, and Mandy climbed in beside him, with Clementine squeezing into the space between them.

"Y'all okay back there?" Rob chuckled as the siblings squirmed and pushed to get comfortable.

"Yessir." They spoke all at once, with Clementine making it a trio.

"Okay, see you at church. Thanks, Lauren, Zoey."

He waited until Lauren made a U-turn and headed back to town before climbing back in the truck and doing the same in the other direction.

"Well, that's something." Mom petted Lady, who had slumped down on her lap. The dog had a few burrs stuck in her coat, and her feet and legs were dusty. Otherwise she looked okay. He'd have to check her out once they got her home.

"What's something?"

"You just sent your kids off with a woman who, a few months ago, you had no use for." She grinned in her annoying way. "Are we seeing a little, um, *romance* developing?"

Rob wasn't about to discuss his confused feelings about

Lauren with Mom. "The only *romance*—" he shuddered as he said the word "—I see developing is between you and that James person." He slid a quick glance toward her. "Don't think I haven't overheard you talking with him on the phone. And it's not all about wallpaper and landscaping."

"Ah. Redirecting the topic, I see." Mom chuckled. "Not to mention eavesdropping."

He returned a cheeky grin. "How else can I find out anything about my family?" He was teasing, of course, but he did have some concerns about this contractor. Maybe he should hire a private investigator to check the man out. Or maybe he could just trust his mother's judgment and let her live her own life.

No, not when he got that thread of worry weaving through him every time she mentioned the man. If James drove up to spend Thanksgiving with them as planned, Rob would grill him like a police detective to be sure he wasn't out for Mom's considerable money. He had a responsibility to guard his family. All of them.

Chapter Thirteen

Seeing Robert park his truck in front of the law office, Lauren couldn't keep the grin from her face. He was smiling, too, as he hopped out and walked toward the front door. This was the second time this week he'd asked her to lunch. Was that why he was here? Over the past two weeks, they'd gotten closer to each other, usually over a meal before Bible study and on Saturdays while the kids were riding.

He poked his head in the door. "Hey. Want to go to lunch with me?"

She inhaled quietly to keep from sounding breathless. "Sure. Give me a minute to finish this document." She forced her concentration back to her computer. She didn't dare make a mistake that would trip Will up when he took this custody case to court.

"No problem. I'll go pester my cousins and check out the improvements in this place." He disappeared around the corner into the new hallway the builders had finished last week.

Lauren's hands refused to cooperate as she continued typing. Which was silly because she'd attended their regular Bible study with him just last night. She needed to get control of her involuntary responses to his presence, even when he surprised her like today.

Eyes on her computer, she heard another person enter the front door. She looked up and briefly couldn't figure out where she'd seen him before. As realization struck, she felt herself moving her rolling chair back toward the wall behind her desk.

"Hello, Lauren." Her ex-husband stood before her, a sardonic grin on his face. "Well, don't you look professional in that granny hairdo and frumpy suit. Looks like the years haven't been all that good to you." He spoke in a low voice, his tone full of intimidation.

After all these years, he still used insults to try to dominate and control her. Heat rushed up her neck and filled her face. Struggling to gather her wits, she swallowed hard and fought against the urge to take out the clip holding up her hair to let it fall over her shoulders. Because he'd always wanted her to wear it that way. His coming here could not be good. But what could he want? Hadn't she already torn out her heart and given it to him on a platter years ago? As she looked closer, she could see he'd had work done on his face, because his skin was altogether too tight for a man his age. But as much as she was tempted to return an insult, she managed to contain it.

"Singleton." She scrambled to recall her old battle plan of how to maintain her self-confidence under the onslaught of his insults. Not one idea came to mind. But then, no matter what she'd ever done, he'd always managed to win. "What brings you here?"

"Right to the point. That's my girl." He smirked, and one corner of his lips lifted in a sneer.

I am not *your girl!* "How did you even find me?" Her voice sounded thin, weak. Oh, how she hated not being able to exhibit strength in the face of this invasion.

"Ah, there you go, proving your ignorance. Did you forget I got my start in investigative journalism? I can still find anybody, anyplace." He laughed in that evil way of his.

"If you have anything to say to me, you could have written a letter. Sent a text. Why did you come all the way out to New Mexico?"

"Get real, Lauren." He glanced toward the hall to the back offices, then placed his fists on her desk and leaned toward her in a menacing posture. "Only a fool would create a paper or text trail. This is between you and me, *Lauren*. Nobody needs to know about our business."

"But—"

"Listen, I don't have time for chitchat." He spoke in a low, threatening tone. "I'm here to tell you I'm running for the US Senate, and I need you to clean up the mess you made of my reputation. Some smart-aleck reporter dug up info about our divorce, so I need a statement from you saying you instigated our separation and abandoned me. Took our poor, disabled child and left for parts unknown. For the sake of my campaign, I need to take Jody—"

"Jody? You don't even know your own daughter's name." Terror smothered her, making it hard to breathe. "You signed away your parental rights—" She had the paperwork packed away in a locked file box back at the apartment, but would that be enough? With Singleton, she had no idea what devious tricks he might pull. He certainly knew the right people to back up his claims, and he could afford the best big-city lawyers.

"Lauren?" Robert returned to the reception area, with Sam and Will right behind him. Lined up shoulder to shoulder, the three formed a formidable group. "Who's this?"

Singleton's entire demeanor changed. Suddenly he was the affable news anchor and, apparently, the budding politician. He stepped over to the Mattson cousins and reached out to Robert, but Robert pulled back instead of shaking his hand. That didn't faze Singleton.

"Singleton Weatherby Parker. Glad to meet you. Nice little place you have here." He waved a hand around the modest office. "Just right for a small town. Clean and tidy and not too showy."

"What do you want?" Scowling at him, all three cousins seemed to speak at once.

Singleton took a step back. The shock on his overworked face made her laugh, releasing the tension in her chest almost on a sob.

Robert stepped over to her and put his arm around her waist in a brotherly way, much like Pastor Tim did with the older folks he wanted to encourage. "You okay?"

For a single beat, she longed to melt into his protective arms. But this was her battle. The only way to win it was to fight it herself. Before she could speak, Sam posted his fists at his waist.

"Yeah, Lauren," he said. "Is this dude bothering you?"

"No. Yes." She struggled to speak, to be very careful of what she said. If she played this wrong, Singleton might actually find a way to take Zoey away from her. "This is my ex-husband. He wants to take Zo...my daughter."

"Yeah, I heard." Robert gave her another little side hug, then moved toward Singleton and towered over him. "Listen, buddy, you need to back off. Her daughter's not going anyplace, especially not with a man who doesn't even know her name and who's denied her existence for the better part of fifteen years."

Singleton collected himself, as Lauren had seen him do many times when he felt threatened, and straightened to his six-foot height, which still fell short of Robert's imposing stature. "Do you have any idea who I am?" This was new. He rarely let his carefully constructed facade slip.

"Yeah, I know who you are," Robert drawled, sounding like the legendary TV Western marshal getting ready to throw the shady gambler out of Dodge. "The question is, do you know who *I* am?"

"Sure, cowboy. You're this woman's latest boyfri—"

Robert grabbed Singleton's shirt and tie and pulled him up nose to nose. "This *lady* is a decent, hardworking single mother who this community cares deeply about. So you need to hightail it back to your little television station and don't bother to come back *or* try to contact her again." He gave Singleton a little shove. "You got that?"

Singleton straightened his tie and tugged at his shirt cuffs. Lauren could practically see the steam coming out of his ears. She didn't know whether to laugh or cry. "Robert, I—"

"Don't worry, Lauren." He held up a hand. "I've got this." He faced Singleton again. "I said, you got that?"

Still working his cuffs, a nervous gesture Lauren had never seen before, Singleton said, "I hardly think you have anything real to threaten me with—"

Robert held up his hand, palm out like a stop sign. Singleton flinched and stepped back.

Robert pulled his phone from his pocket and punched it. "Rex, I've got some fella here at my cousins' law office who's threatening Lauren. I think he needs to cool his heels in your jail. I'll hold on to him until you get here. Good. See you soon."

Lauren glanced at Will and Sam, whose expressions showed the same determination as Robert's, like a posse of good guys staring down an outlaw. Singleton's artificially tanned face turned white around the edges, and his jaw slackened.

Somehow Lauren managed to hold in the giddy laugh trying to escape her. Nothing about this scene was funny. But why couldn't her resolve gain any traction? Why was she letting Robert and her bosses manage the situation? Didn't they realize Singleton would only come back at her when she was alone? She had to fight this herself.

Robert punched his phone again. "Hey, Marty. Rob Mattson here. Listen, I need you to get Zoey Parker down to the school office and keep her there with our school resource officer. Don't let anybody, any strangers, talk to her. Tell her everything's okay so she won't worry. Good. Thanks."

Zoey *would* worry! She'd be terrified! Lauren tried to protest, but the words wouldn't form.

Rob punched his phone a third time. "Hey, George. Rob Mattson here. I need you to bring your photographer over to the law office. We've got a good story for the front page of the *Riverton Journal*. Good. See you soon."

He disconnected the call and gave Singleton a warning look. "Does that answer your question about who I am?"

Singleton glared at Robert, then Will, then Sam, finally settling an arrogant grin in Lauren's direction. "You haven't heard the last from me." He walked toward the door. She didn't have a single doubt that he meant it.

Sam reached the door first and placed his palm against it. "Just cool your heels, pilgrim." He did his best imitation of a famous Western movie hero. "The sheriff'll be right over, along with the editor and photog from the paper."

"You have no right to hold me here." Singleton's voice sounded a little reedy, not at all like his eloquent on-screen news delivery. "And no authority."

The next few minutes proved him wrong. Sheriff Blake arrived, sat him down and questioned him, with Robert correcting him when he tried to lie, while George took notes and Bill took photos.

"Now, Mr. Weatherby Parker—" the sheriff spoke in a paternal tone "—you just skedaddle back to your little television job and your political campaign. I can't wish you well in either because you ain't the kind of man we should have in the news service or in public office." He cleared his throat. "And if you decide to cause any more trouble for our Miss Lauren, you can be sure we'll let everybody, and I do mean *everybody* here and in Florida, know exactly what sort of man you really are."

"Aw, Sheriff," George grumbled, "do you mean I can't run this story on the front page tonight and send it out to all the news services?" There was a twinkle in his eye as he spoke.

"Naw, better not. At least not yet. Let's give ol' Singleton here a chance to do the right thing and get outta Dodge with his tail between his legs. But we'll hold on to that story and those pictures in case he tries to cause Miss Lauren any trouble in the future." The sheriff eyed Singleton up and down. "You got that?" At Singleton's weak nod, he added, "You can go, Senator Wannabe." Sheriff Blake opened the door and shoved Singleton's shoulder perhaps a little too forcefully.

Trying to regather his dignity, he strode from the office, but was clearly shaken, because he stumbled on the uneven pavement and barely managed to regain his balance before hurrying away toward a fancy new car parked out front, no doubt a rental.

While her protectors guffawed at Singleton's awkward re-treat, Lauren dropped into her chair and covered her face, finally surrendering to tears.

Robert knelt beside her. "Hey, honey, don't cry. He can't hurt you. I'll...we'll make sure of that."

She barely registered his use of *honey*. He didn't have a clue what she was thinking. Couldn't he see that he was just like Singleton? Taking over her life and making decisions for her? But it wouldn't do to alienate him, not when he must be seeing himself as some sort of hero. Oh, she was so foolish. He *was* a hero. Just one she didn't want in this situation.

She looked up at him and gave him a wobbly smile. "I know. It's just that—" *Think fast, Lauren!* "—just that I've never told Zoey very much about her father. Now I'll have to tell her everything. She's going to be devastated."

For maybe the second time in his life, Rob had used his family name and position in the community to take control of a bad situation. If he'd given in to his first impulse when he heard Lauren's ex belittling her, he would have pummeled that narcissistic manipulator into the ground. But that would have reduced Rob to Parker's level and probably reduced him in Lauren's eyes. The sweet smile on her pretty face, if a little strained right now, made his self-control all the more rewarding.

"Don't worry, sweetheart." He couldn't seem to keep from using fond names for her. If she didn't like it, she didn't show it. "Zoey's a smart girl. She'll understand."

"You don't know that." She mumbled the words.

He couldn't blame her for having natural concerns about her child, but he'd make sure Zoey was safe. Behind him, he heard the others start to disperse, their part in rescuing her complete.

"Thank you." She looked around him. "Thank you all for your help."

Rex touched the brim of his hat, which he'd probably kept on to reinforce his authority in front of Parker. "You're welcome, Miss Lauren. You let us know if he even calls you—"

"Or texts you," said George, a younger man. "Or tries to contact you on any social media."

"Right." The sheriff nodded. "You'd know about all that stuff."

"Rob, Lauren, I'll text you the pictures." Bill held up his camera. "After I download them."

"Thanks, guys." Rob stood and shook hands with the three men who'd come running at his call. "Let me know if I can return the favor."

Will and Sam had already gone back to their offices, but soon emerged wearing their hats and winter vests.

"Let us take you to lunch." Will beckoned to Lauren.

"Oh, I—"

"She's going with me." Rob took her fleece jacket from the coatrack in the corner behind her desk and held it for her. Glancing down, he noticed the jacket's frayed cuffs and worn sleeves. Maybe he could get Mom to pick out a new coat for her. Or maybe he should take her over to the mall and buy one for her right now. "You should give her the rest of the day off so she can see about Zoey, okay?"

"I don't need the day off." Sounding annoyed, Lauren stepped back, not accepting his help into the coat. What was that all about? "I'm going to the school now to bring Zoey back here." She looked at his cousins. "Is that okay?"

"Sure," Will and Sam said together. Funny how these guys were almost like the twins. Probably because they were close in age and grew up together. Now, if they could just catch his drift that he had this under control.

"We should have lunch first so you can have a chance to get past all this stuff before you talk to Zoey." Rob again lifted the coat for her. "Here. It's pretty cold outside."

"No. I'm going to the school." She snatched the coat from him and put it on herself.

He couldn't quite read her expression, but it sure didn't look like gratitude. "Don't you want some backup?"

Lauren glared up at him, and a memory flashed through his mind. That was the way Jordyn had looked at him when he forbade her to train Rowdy. *Uh-oh...*

"Time for us to make our exit." Will headed for the door, Sam right on his heels. "Lauren, don't forget to lock up."

Once they were outside, she huffed out a cross sigh. "As if I would forget." She grabbed up her purse and walked to the door. "You going?"

Rob stared at her for a moment. "Yeah. You sure you don't want me—"

"No." She held the door open, despite the brisk wind sweeping in, and tapped her foot on the floor. "Any time, cowboy."

Ouch. "Are you mad at me?"

"Yes. No." She gave his arm a little shove. "I really need to get to Zoey."

"Sure." He stepped out the door. "Are you sure you don't want me—"

"No. Thank you." She shut the door and punched in the lock code, then marched toward the parking lot beside the building.

Rob stared after her. *What in the world just happened?*

* * *

Robert is not Singleton!

Lauren tried to hammer that thought into her brain, but it wasn't working. Of course she wasn't being fair. Despite his earlier suspicions, Robert had never, not even once, belittled her. Then again, Singleton hadn't, either, when they'd first met. Not until she'd fallen for his charming romantic advances did he start criticizing everything she did, said or wore. Her brother had warned her to drop him, but their parents thought Singleton was perfect in every way. And Lauren had been so enthralled with the up-and-coming news anchor that she refused to heed her brother's warnings.

Not that Robert was making romantic moves toward her. Their lives simply intersected in many ways. She worked for his cousins. They attended the same church. Most important, he'd been helpful with Zoey, letting his twins teach her to ride and sticking around to make sure she was safe. Yes, they'd gone out to lunch and dinner a few times. Yes, they'd found a common interest in the Bible study. But that didn't mean they were in a relationship, as she'd been with Singleton all those years ago, when it had been a terrible mistake to rely on her youthful feelings.

The best way to avoid making another mistake was to avoid Robert Mattson…if only she could do that without putting an end to Zoey's riding lessons or the other times she spent with Mandy and Bobby. After all of the challenges Zoey had faced and did face, Lauren couldn't bring herself to cut off the first real friendships her daughter ever had. She also didn't want to stop attending the Bible study because what she learned was deepening her faith. But she could go by herself.

Zoey was waiting for her in the office with shaking hands and stuttering speech that revealed her anxiety. "M-Mom, wh-what happened?"

"Don't worry, honey." Lauren signed the sheet offered by

the school secretary. "Thanks, Marty. Let's go, Zoey." She then nodded to the school resource officer, a muscular, sixty-something man. "Thank you."

"Just doing my job, ma'am." His paternal smile reminded her of Robert's warm concern for Zoey.

She drove through the fast-food restaurant and bought lunch and milkshakes for both of them. She would make chicken and dumplings for supper, more comfort food, probably more for herself than for Zoey.

They arrived at the office before her bosses. Inside, she spread out their food on her desk and managed to say a feeble prayer of thanks. She looked up to see Zoey staring at her.

"Mom, what's going on? Why'd you have me called to the office?" She sniffed back tears. "I was so scared something happened to you."

"As you can see, I'm fine." Lauren forced a cheerful tone. "Eat your chicken nuggets." She dunked one in the honey mustard sauce and took a bite. "Mm. Delicious, as always."

"Mom..." Zoey leveled her gaze on Lauren, a new maturity shining in her eyes. "Don't treat me like a baby. Miss Marty got me out of class and made me sit in the office with Deputy Garrett. She didn't tell me why. You think I'm not going to worry?"

Lauren exhaled a long sigh. This was Robert's fault. Didn't he know nobody could take a student from the school without a parent's signed permission? Zoey had been safe at her classroom. But then, who knew what Singleton could have done? Might still do? Now Lauren was forced to tell her daughter the whole story about her father, something she'd dreaded for years.

At twenty-three months, Zoey failed to meet the usual milestones of healthy infant maturing and was subsequently diagnosed as having cerebral palsy, so Singleton wanted to put her in a care home away from public view. When Lauren refused, he left them. And ever since the divorce, which she did not contest, well-meaning people who thought Singleton hung the moon had warned her never to criticize him to Zoey. Because, everybody said, that would unfairly alienate the child from the absent parent. Or, on the other hand, cause the child to defend him even though she never knew him. So, how could she give her daughter an accurate picture of Singleton?

"Sweetie." Lauren took Zoey's hand. "A man came here to the office today." She inhaled deeply. "He's your father."

Zoey gasped, and her eyes widened with fear. "Wh-what did he want?"

This wasn't the response Lauren had expected. "He…he wanted to meet you and take you back to—"

"I don't want to meet him." Uncharacteristic hurt and a hint of anger shone in Zoey's eyes.

"I'm glad to hear that. Can you tell me why?"

Zoey rolled her eyes and gave her that teenage look questioning her mother's intelligence. "Mom, do you think all last summer when I stayed home alone I wouldn't look through your stuff?" She gave Lauren a cute little grin. "I figured you were hiding something from me, and I found your divorce papers." Her expression shone with hurt again. "And I found those papers my father…*that man* signed saying he gave away his parental rights so he didn't have to pay child support. And that was just two years ago. Now I understand why we didn't have much money since then." She smirked. "What kind of name is Singleton, anyway?"

Lauren chuckled. That's what Robert had said. And she couldn't be cross with Zoey for snooping. She should have realized her natural curiosity would prompt this search. And she should have told Zoey about Singleton long ago rather than deflecting all of her daughter's questions about who her father was. Instead, she'd arranged all the paperwork to be finalized while her daughter was in school. She never told Zoey her father was ashamed of her, that he wanted to deny her existence until it became politically expedient for him to trot her out for show, all the while making Lauren the villain.

"My sweet girl, I wish I could tell you he had some redeeming quality, but…" Lauren stopped before she said something really bad that might come back later and hurt them both.

"You know what I figured out?" Zoey snickered. "After I read all that stuff, I thought, hey, even Genghis Khan had kids. The important thing is Jesus loves me and accepts me just as I am. I'm His child. Knowing that, believing that is what's important."

Count on this remarkable girl to turn to God, whatever the situation.

"Hey, did Mandy's dad tell you about the Riverton Fall Festival two weekends from this Saturday?"

Zoey was ready to move on to another subject, so Lauren let the matter drop. When it was convenient, she would explain more about Singleton's political plans and how he'd wanted to use his rejected daughter to ramp up his social and street cred…at Lauren's expense, of course.

"Yes, I think it was mentioned." Recalling how she'd acted toward Robert after he sent her ex packing, she knew an apology was in order. "Want to go?"

"*Duh.* Corn dogs, cotton candy, pumpkin pie–eating competitions, carnival rides. What's not to like?" Zoey giggled. "This Saturday after my riding lesson, Bobby's gonna show me how Lady's doing with her herding lessons. They practice before and after school every day, and his dad wants him to enter in the calf herding competition."

"That'll be fun." For Robert's sake, and Bobby's, Lauren hoped, even prayed, Lady could be retrained for the job she was meant to have.

But even as she lifted her silent prayer, she knew her real hope and dream was that Zoey could adopt Lady as her companion and, after Singleton's threats, her protector.

Yeah, that wasn't going to happen.

Chapter Fourteen

"**D**ad, you know I can't whistle." Bobby scowled at Rob as they stood inside the pasture fence, with their three dogs sitting nearby and a dozen or so yearling steers grazing on the autumn stubble of grass. "How'm I supposed to signal Lady when my lips won't cooperate?"

Before Rob could answer, Mandy piped up from her seat on the top fence rail. "It's easy." She put her fingers to her lips and let out an ear-piercing sound, and all three border collies perked up their ears and looked at her, waiting further instructions. "See?" She jumped down and grabbed Bobby's left hand. "Just hold your fingers like this." She tried to show him, but he pulled away. Shrugging, she repeated the shrill sound, and the dogs stood up on the alert.

Bobby glared at her. "Sis, you know I've been trying to whistle since we were kids. It just comes out like a sick wheeze."

Since we were kids? Like you're all grown-up now. Rob chuckled despite his annoyance. This exercise wasn't working according to plan, although he had to give Bobby credit for trying to master the skill even though his heart wasn't in it. But given enough time, he was bound to change his mind.

"Okay, son. Tell you what. I'll dig out my old whistle, and we'll try again this evening after football practice. You need to keep working with Lady before the contest so you can at least make a showing." Rob's hopes of his son being a champion dog trainer would have to wait, but maybe entering the herding event would stir up a sense of competition in Bobby, something oddly lacking considering his heritage. "You two go flag down the school bus to get to school. I'll work with Lady for a little while." He escorted them out through the gate.

While Lady followed the kids out of the pasture, Scotch and Irish trotted over to him, their tilted heads asking why he wasn't putting them to work with the steers. The two older dogs didn't need practice, but Lady would require some serious work. At the rate Bobby was going, Rob would have to spend a lot of time with her himself, then turn her instruction over to Bobby.

"How about me, Daddy?" Clementine climbed down from the fence. "Do I get to stay home today?" She gave him a sassy grin.

"Hey, kiddo. Didn't see you there." He patted her head, careful not to mess up the ponytail Mom had arranged. He'd have to depend on Mandy to take care of her little sister's hair after Mom moved to Phoenix. He'd miss all the help she'd given him with the kids since Jordyn's death, but mostly he'd miss her. He wasn't looking forward to meeting that fella she kept talking about who was working on her condo. He still might hire a PI to investigate him.

The kids grabbed their backpacks from beside the fence and dashed toward the front gate as the yellow school bus rounded a distant curve. He watched as they flagged it down and climbed aboard, then returned to the pasture. They were growing up too fast, but not so fast that he didn't want to keep an eye on them. Wasn't that the job, the privilege of every parent? Well, maybe not *every* parent.

The memory of Lauren's ex threatening to take Zoey away from her brought a burst of anger to Rob's chest. Then he remembered her angrily dismissing him, making clear her feelings for him. Okay, he could deal with that. He could back off and let her be. On the other hand, after learning about and meeting that Singleton dude, Rob figured her ex was the dark secret he'd thought she was hiding. Another doubt about her character fell away. He hadn't known her for long, but the walls were coming down. Not that she'd ever shown interest in him beyond friendship.

It'd been different with Jordyn, the only woman beside his mother and sister he'd ever been close to. They'd grown up together and gone steady since middle school. No matter how much Rob examined his memories or beat himself up over this, he would never understand why she'd gone behind his back and tried to train Rowdy. What had she needed to prove? And to whom?

Forgive.

The word seemed to come out of nowhere.

Forgive.

It grew louder in his mind, and he slumped against the pasture fence. "Lord, is that what I need to do? Even if I'll never have the answers about Jordyn's deception?"

Forgive.

"All right. I get it." He lifted his gaze to the clear blue morning sky. "Lord, I don't know if Jordyn can hear me, but if not, please pass this on to her. Darlin', I'll never stop missing you, but I forgive you." More conviction grew in his chest. "I know you're with the Lord, so you've probably already forgiven me for failing you." A rush of memories came to mind.

Jordyn on their wedding day, too beautiful for words. Jordyn on bed rest until the twins were born, then pushing through exhaustion when they came down with childhood illnesses. Jordyn weeping over the two babies that didn't make it to full term. Jordyn when Clementine came out all red and howling and determined to live. Mostly, Jordyn, sweet, understanding and supportive as Rob endeavored every day, every hour to live up to his family's hundred-and-forty-year legacy. But what had she done for herself?

Daughter of a world-class bull-riding champion, she'd been a fierce, fearless barrel racer and beautiful rodeo queen. After they married, it took several years for the kids to come along. When they did, at Rob's insistence, she'd given up her own pursuits to stay home and take care of them. Had she longed for something more? If so, no wonder she didn't tell him what she was doing. Yes, she'd disobeyed his orders, something none of his ranch hands would ever do. But she wasn't a hired hand. She was his wife. His partner. His equal. If he'd been less heavy-handed, maybe she would have trusted him enough to tell him she wanted to train Rowdy so she could get back into barrel racing. If only they'd talked. If only he'd listened. He could have helped her choose a different horse. He should have— Then it hit him. Her death was as much his fault as hers.

For the first time since Jordyn's funeral, Rob broke down and wept, leaning his arms on the top fence rail and resting his head on his forearm as tears dampened his long shirtsleeves.

Scotch and Irish lay on the ground nearby and watched him, heads still tilted in their questioning way. But Lady nudged up against his leg. When he reached down to pet her, she licked his hand. He knelt and pulled her into his arms. This little gal sure did have a special instinct for human needs. She licked his cheek, then rested her head against his chest. With that contact, he felt a comfort, a brief respite from his grief. He held Lady close, and she let him.

He'd always had dogs, had been close to several of them. Only one had responded to his emotions this way, but she hadn't been a border collie, just a bedraggled mutt that wandered in off the prairie when Rob was about ten years old. He'd nursed Lottie back to health, and she'd been devoted to him.

Had waited by the front fence every day until he came home from school and followed him everywhere around the ranch.

No wonder Lady wanted to be with Zoey so much that she'd followed her back to the apartment two weeks ago. Last spring, Zoey and Lauren rescued Lady and nursed her back to health. She'd bonded with them in a way she never had with Bobby, even as a puppy.

Rob released a long sigh. Did that mean he had to give up on Bobby and turn his expensive herding dog over to Zoey? Could Lauren even afford the healthy dog food Lady required? And what about Lady being shut up in that apartment every day while Zoey went to school and Lauren worked?

No, that wasn't a good idea. He needed to stick with his plans. He would work with Bobby and Lady before and after school every day until the Riverton Fall Festival competition. He didn't want Lady to lose her nurturing skills, but she could learn to do so much more than be a lay-about companion. On a ranch, everybody worked, even the barn cats, so Lady simply had to learn how to do her job.

"Hey, cowboy." Lauren sidled up to Robert as he supervised the kids while they tacked up Tripper and two other horses. Ready to eat humble pie, she wasn't sure how to begin.

"Howdy, ma'am." He touched the brim of his hat and gave her a welcoming, teasing smile, dimple and all, which almost threw her off course.

She could stare at this good-looking man all day. Instead, she managed, "Look, I'm really sorry for being cross with you the other day."

"Hey, no problem. You were worried about Zoey." The soft, understanding look in his eyes warmed her heart and dispelled her anxiety about the situation.

"And thanks for sticking up for me, Marshal Dillon." She enjoyed his deep chuckle for a moment. "And for chasing the bad guy out of Dodge." She glanced at the kids, but they weren't paying attention to this conversation.

"Wellll," Robert drawled, "truth be told, I can't take all the credit, Miss Lauren. It was Sheriff Blake who made that varmint skedaddle."

She loved this new banter. "That's true, but not till you rounded up a posse to back him up."

"Aw, shucks, ma'am—"

"Ready to go, Dad." Mandy had Zoey up in the saddle, and she and Bobby were ready to mount their own horses. "Miss Lauren, is it okay for us to ride around the ranch a bit? We won't go far or fast."

"And we'll stay on the flat land," Bobby added.

Her focus swiftly shifting, Lauren walked over to Tripper and studied her daughter's smiling face. "You okay up there?"

"Yes, ma'am. Are you?" Zoey glanced at Robert and smirked.

So she'd been paying more attention than Lauren had thought. "Yes, smarty-pants. I'm fine. You be careful. Let Mandy or Bobby know if you sense anything happening." She gave her a meaningful glance.

Zoey rolled her eyes. "I know." She reached up and adjusted her helmet strap. "I don't want to fall even more than you don't want me to, y'know."

Lauren squeezed Zoey's hand. "I know."

Oh, how hard it was to let go of her not-so-little girl. As the kids rode out of the barn at a slow pace, with Lady trotting alongside Tripper and keeping her eyes on Zoey, she sent up a silent prayer for their safety.

"Want to saddle up and ride with them?"

Robert's question in her ear sent a nice little shiver down her side. She had to inhale a quick breath before she could answer.

"Let's just watch from here."

He chuckled. "Still not ready to ride?"

She glanced up, enjoying his teasing grin. "Nope."

"Okay, then. But one day."

"Uh-huh." In truth, she would like to give it a try. But what if she fell off and broke an arm? How would she take care of Zoey or work at the law firm? No, that kind of fun would have to wait until Zoey no longer needed her. Besides, Robert's attention should be on the kids, not her…although she didn't mind in the least the dimpled smiles he kept sending her way.

Seated in the bleachers at the Riverton Fairgrounds arena the following Saturday, Rob watched as Bobby entered the field with Lady. The dog had been excited to greet Zoey when she and Lauren arrived at the fairgrounds. But once Zoey sent her back to Bobby, he managed to keep her at his side. Now Zoey and Lauren sat with Rob and his family, waiting for their boy and his dog to compete. Before and after school, Bobby had practiced diligently with Lady, using the whistle Rob provided, and now he could command his dog by varying the pitch and length of each signal.

Bobby's pal Josh Moberly, from a neighboring ranch, put his dog through his paces. Scout ran close to the ground and stared into the face of the steer he was to cut from the herd. At Josh's signal, he ran to its left side to direct it to the right. The steer tried to go left, but Scout was all up in its face, getting between it and the other animals. Within seconds, the steer ran toward the chute at the end of the arena with Scout chasing all the way. The dog then ran back to crouch by Josh's side and await his next command.

Rob's excitement grew as he waited for Lady to perform just as perfectly. They stepped into position and waited for the judge's signal as the crowd grew quiet. Except for one voice… Zoey's.

"Go, Lady!"

Lady perked up her ears, then dashed away from Bobby,

squeezed through the end of the gate and headed for the stands. Before Bobby could figure out what was happening, Lady was at Zoey's side, wagging her tail and looking for a treat.

"Oh, no, Lady." Zoey laughed, but her face was flushed. "Go back to Bobby. It's your turn to herd those cows." She tried to wave her away. "Oh, I'm so sorry, Mr. Mattson." She cast a worried glance at Rob. "Lady, go back to Bobby." Tears started to form in her eyes.

"Don't worry, kiddo." Rob didn't want her to get too upset over this. "There's always next time."

"I'm sorry, too." Seated beside him, Lauren gave him a sympathetic smile. "We shouldn't have come."

"Don't say that." Rob squeezed her hand. Bobby should have grabbed Lady's collar when she started to bolt.

He glanced toward the arena, where his son was jogging toward the gate. Despite Lady's breaking form and thereby disqualifying them both, he didn't look disappointed. No surprise there. Rob had enough disappointment for them both.

"Hey, don't worry, son. A little more work, and you and Lady will do better next spring."

"Thanks, Dad." Bobby petted Lady. "Good girl." He dug a treat from his pocket and gave it to the dog.

Rob groaned inside. He shouldn't be rewarding Lady when she hadn't done her job. No, that was wrong. Depriving the dog wasn't the way to train her or win her allegiance. Besides, Rob could see Lady had no idea she'd done something wrong.

After others competed, Josh and Scout won the blue ribbon. With Mom, Lauren and the kids all chatting about the other Fall Festival events, Rob had no choice but to set aside his disappointment about Lady and try to enjoy the rest of the day. It was time for him to have a serious talk with Lauren, so he'd invited her to dinner this evening. A nervous thread wound through his chest. When the time came, would he have the courage to tell her what he'd been thinking about?

* * *

"Are you sure you'll be okay?" Lauren resisted the urge to hold on to Zoey as her daughter prepared to climb into Andrea's truck. She'd never been on a sleepover, and Lauren had been reluctant to let her accept Mandy's invitation.

"Mo-o-m." Zoey whispered her complaint. "I'll be fine. Just go."

"She'll be fine," Andrea echoed as she gave Lauren a side hug. "We'll swing by your apartment and get her pj's and Sunday clothes. Oh, and her meds. I can call you if she needs anything else. You just enjoy your evening out." She glanced at Robert, who was leaning against the side of the pickup, arms crossed. "Go on."

Zoey had already climbed into the truck and made herself comfortable beside Mandy and Lady. The dog plunked her head down on Zoey's lap as though the day had worn her out. They'd been inseparable since the herding competition, with Lady walking beside Zoey around the midway and Clementine tagging along beside them. Lauren had noticed Lady seemed attached to the little girl, because she wouldn't let her stray far from the family group. If only those judges could see the way Lady "herded" these two kids, they'd give her a ribbon.

"Ready?" Robert gave her one of his gorgeous, dimpled smiles. "Don't know about you, but all this walking's made me hungry."

Lauren returned a smile. "So those four hot dogs and all that cotton candy didn't hold you?"

"Hey, I only had two hot dogs and one stick of cotton candy." Robert took her elbow and guided her toward his pickup, parked several spaces away. "Anyway, I always have room for a steak."

He seemed pretty happy despite Lady's disappointing behavior. Lauren wouldn't bring it up though. That would ruin this lovely evening before it started.

"After all that walking, I could eat, too." She gave him an impish grin. "But I'm hungry for grilled salmon or maybe chicken Alfredo."

He put a hand on his chest. "Wow, you sure know how to hurt a cattleman's heart." He opened the front passenger door and helped her climb in. "Might as well do drive-through and get chicken nuggets."

Before she could respond, he shut the door and jogged around to the driver's side like a man half his age. Once behind the wheel, he again gave her that smile that tickled her heart. "So, what'll it be?"

"Oh, well." She exhaled a long sigh. "Guess it'll have to be steak."

His warm chuckle rumbled clear down in his chest. "Smart lady."

Truth was she loved the steaks at his family's restaurant. So that's what she ordered once they were seated across from each other in a back booth. As always, the aromas of grilled steaks and freshly made bread wafted through the air, inciting her appetite.

"So, how did you feel about—"

"I wanted to talk with you about—"

They spoke at the same time, then laughed.

"You go first." Lauren doubted he wanted to discuss Lady's behavior, so she was glad he spoke up. "What did you want to talk to me about?"

"Not *to* you." He nodded to the server, who'd just brought their sweet tea and complimentary rolls and cornbread to the table. "*With* you."

"Oh." Must be something about the kids. "Okay. Shoot."

He buttered a piece of cornbread and took a bite, so she followed suit. The spicy morsel, seasoned with onions, corn and jalapeño peppers, melted in her mouth.

"Wow. This is so good." She buttered another bite. "What did you want to say?"

He took a deep breath, almost like he was gathering courage. What on earth?

"Lauren, at the risk of sounding like an awkward teenage boy, I—I'd like to know where you see our relationship—" he cleared his throat "—our *friend*ship going."

A crumb of cornbread stuck in her throat, and she coughed so hard, Robert came around the table to pound her back.

She held up a hand. "I'm okay." She took a long drink of her tea, then laughed. "Whew! That was not a commentary on the cornbread."

"Glad to hear it." He took his seat again and gazed at her, his question still in his eyes.

"So, you want a DTR conversation?" She managed not to laugh at the confusion on his face. "Define the relationship?"

"Ah." Another smile. "Yeah. That."

She could look into that handsome face all evening and never tire of the way the candlelight reflected in his ice-blue eyes. "Well, where do you think it's going?"

Her ex's domineering behavior notwithstanding, she still held on to the old-fashioned idea that a man should state his feelings first.

"I like being with you. You're easy to talk to. Good with the kids. Get along with my mom. That's a big one." He chuckled as he reached across the wide table and briefly touched her hand. "I like *you*, Lauren. A lot."

She swallowed hard, and it had nothing to do with the cornbread. "I like you, too, Robert."

He continued to look at her expectantly. What else did he want her to say?

"I like your whole family. You've all been so kind and generous to Zoey. And me."

He gave a little shrug. "You and Zoey are special to us."

"Thanks." Even though a warm feeling blossomed in her heart and spread up to her face, she was glad he hadn't said he loved her. Especially since she couldn't quite define her own feelings for him. "You're all special to us, too."

"Y'know, since this afternoon, I've been thinking." He buttered another bite of cornbread. "Maybe Zoey should start training Lady to herd cattle. I could teach her."

Wow. This was a rapid change of subject. But she didn't mind. Robert was offering to help her daughter develop her motor skills in a new and challenging way. Almost like a father would do. No, she must not think of it that way.

"How would that work? I mean, doesn't Lady need someone to practice with her every day? I'm not sure we could get out to the ranch that often." Even as she said the words, she tried to think of ways to make it happen.

"Have you noticed that little pink adobe cottage next to Andy's house?"

She lifted one eyebrow. "You mean that large, gorgeous hacienda?"

"That's the one." He grinned. "Nobody's living there right now. Maybe you and Zoey could move out there. It's fully furnished." His grin softened into a warm smile. "Rent-free, of course, because Zoey would be working for us." He paused while the server set their steaks in front of them. "Thanks." Then to Lauren murmured, "Let's pray."

He touched her hand again and bowed his head. "Lord, thank You for Your provision and for the many blessings You bestow on us. Thank You for Lauren and Zoey coming into our lives. Please give us wisdom as our friendship grows."

Lauren had difficulty swallowing her first bite of steak. It was tender and delicious, but her heart was already in her throat. *Yes, Lord, please give wisdom.* Would she be foolish to move out to the ranch? Would it even be proper, with Andrea moving to Phoenix after Christmas? And rent-free? Despite his claim that Zoey would be earning their keep, it sounded too much like charity. It had been one thing for her dad to charge her a reduced rent back in Orlando, but he was family, while Robert was... Hmm. They still had yet to define their relationship. Just how far did he want this to go?

How far did *she* want it to go? The last thing she and Zoey needed was for her to make another poor choice in the romance department. Moving out to the ranch might be the best thing that ever happened to them. But it also might be the worst decision she'd ever made since marrying Singleton.

Chapter Fifteen

Way to kill a conversation, Rob. He wanted to kick himself. He'd wanted to get closer to Lauren through a friendly conversation, but he'd gotten off track, something he rarely did. This lady did that to him. Made him forget what he was doing. Was that good or not so good?

He could see her surprise and maybe a hint of alarm when he brought up moving out to the ranch. He hadn't even thought it through. The words just came out, the idea seeming like the logical solution to having Zoey train Lady. But was such a move wise? What if their relationship didn't grow the way he'd begun to hope it would? Having Lauren live so close could get awkward. But he wouldn't retract his suggestion that Zoey should train Lady. Whatever the logistics of the plan, he felt sure she'd do a good job, and maybe it would be good for her, too.

As for Bobby, Rob could no longer ignore the fact that his son would prefer to play with the dogs rather than train them. Now Rob would need to interest him in some other important part of running the ranch before it was too late. Once he went off to college, he'd major in whatever he wanted, no matter what Rob's plans for him were. In grade school, both he and Mandy had raised steers as their 4-H projects, but he'd lost interest while Mandy continued. She was the one who knew all the ins and outs of the ranch. Took to it like a duck to water. Maybe—

"Would you like some dessert?" Their server stood beside their table, dessert menus in hand.

Rob shook off his musings and looked across the table at Lauren to see she'd finished her small ribeye steak. "Dessert?"

"Sure. I can just hear that chocolate cheesecake calling my name." She smiled in her cute, teasing way. "How about you, cowboy?"

He felt a little kick in his chest every time she called him cowboy. Just one more appealing way she affected him. "I'll take the salty caramel cookie. With ice cream. Make that vanilla."

"Coming right up." The server, a senior from the high school, glanced between Rob and Lauren, then sent him a sassy grin and a quick lift of her eyebrows. "Y'all behave now, Mr. Mattson." She dashed away before he could respond.

Okay, if even a teenage server, who was probably into romance books and movies, could see something was happening here, maybe Rob could get the conversation back on track with his original plan.

"Lauren—"

"Robert—"

"You go first this time. Wait. Why do you always call me Robert? Everybody else calls me Rob."

"Not your mother." She shrugged. "And she was the one who named you."

"Nope. I come from a long line of Robert Mattsons. She didn't have a choice."

"Ah. I see." She flashed him a teasing grin. "Okay, I'll call you Rob."

He chuckled. "No. I like that you call me Robert."

She rolled her eyes like Mandy often did. "You're so funny. Make up your mind."

This wasn't going the way he'd hoped. "Can we get back to, what did you call it, our DTR?"

She blinked. "O-okay. So, how do you define our relationship? Our friendship? Whatever you want to call it."

"I think I'd like for you to be part of my life. Well, you already are, but… I'm not saying this too well." Jordyn used to fill in what he couldn't say, but they'd known each other since childhood. Knew what the other one was thinking without saying a word until she… No, better not go there.

He hadn't known Lauren for long. How did he learn more without being intrusive? Might as well give it a try. "I want to know you better. To know what makes you tick beyond being a really good mom to a very special daughter. And, apparently, an outstanding paralegal for my cousins."

She shrugged. "What you see is what you get." Her face reddened. "I mean I am what you see. Nothing more."

"I like what I see." He gave her what he hoped was an encouraging smile. "The problem I'm having is I think I like you too much."

She stared at him for a moment, her pretty lips quirking to one side. "I don't know whether to be flattered or insulted."

"Ugh. I told you I'm not saying this well." He inhaled a deep breath. "I sure don't mean to either flatter or insult you. Just telling you how I feel." He offered a sheepish grin. "Do you think this clumsy-tongued cowboy has a chance of—" What? What did he want from her? "—of seeing where this all goes?"

The sweet smile on her beautiful face gave him the answer he was hoping for.

Lauren's heart hiccuped. She already loved spending time with this cowboy. But what if they were rushing things? She didn't dare make another mistake.

"I think we can do that, as long as we don't take it too fast."

"Right." His doubtful expression bloomed into one of pure happiness. "Whew. Glad we have that taken care of."

"There." The server set their desserts in front of them. "That wasn't so hard, was it?"

Lauren eyed her doubtfully. Had she been eavesdropping?

"Hey, kiddo." Robert gave her a stern look. "You better keep this to yourself if you want to keep your job." Then he grinned. "Or maybe I should bribe you with a big tip."

The girl giggled. "Aw, Mr. Mattson, you always give us big tips. But I'll try hard not to say anything. You two just look so…so…"

"Thanks—" Robert looked at her name tag "—Stacy. Keep up the good work."

"Yessir." Grinning, she took a step away.

"And mind your own business."

Still grinning, Stacy left them in peace.

"Well, that was fun." Lauren couldn't imagine what it was going to be like having her name, and Zoey's, linked to the most prominent rancher in the state. "And interesting."

"Yeah." He reclaimed Lauren's hand across the table. "Are you okay?"

"Are you kidding?" Unexpected tears sprang to her eyes. "The man whose company I enjoy so much just told me he feels the same way. I don't think I could be any better."

"Me, either."

Chocolate cheesecake had never tasted so good. Even the much richer caramel cookie Robert fed her across the table only added extra sweetness to the evening, as much for the endearing gesture of sharing as for the taste.

Robert Mattson V wanted to explore their relationship. Was she foolish to imagine a future with him? He was fond of Zoey and interested in helping her develop new skills. Did Lauren dare to dream? A tiny, uncomfortable thread of doubt wound through her mind. She'd lost big-time in the romance department. Did she dare hope for a better result this time?

"So, how do we do this?" She took her last bite of cheesecake. "I mean, what do we tell our families?"

He smiled and shrugged. "If they're anything like Stacy, I don't think we'll have to tell them anything."

At her apartment building, he walked her to the outside door. "Shall I pick you up for church tomorrow?"

"I should drive. Zoey will be tired from the fair and spending the night at your place, and I may need to bring her home right after the service."

"Okay." He kept staring at her as though he wanted to say more.

"I should go in."

"Right." He opened the apartment building's front door, then closed it and gently enfolded her in his strong arms. "Lauren," he whispered into her hair.

Oh, it felt so good to be held that way. So comforting. So... romantic.

He lifted her chin and gazed at her lips. "May I—?"

As much as she longed for him to kiss her, her best instincts said no, not when she still needed to examine that bothersome thread of doubt. Instead, she rose up on tiptoes and kissed his cheek. "Good night." She pulled away and hurried inside before he could say more.

As always, she second-guessed her actions. Should she have let him kiss her? For some reason, as nice as it might have been, she was glad she hadn't. A kiss was a seal, a promise. And they definitely weren't ready for promises. Did he understand that?

Still, his words about their server observing their growing feelings for each other were spot-on. The next day at church, everybody seemed to give them the same knowing smile. Or maybe they smiled because she and Zoey sat with Robert and his family in the middle pew, as though it was something they'd long expected.

Zoey reported that she'd had a great time sleeping over with Mandy. Mandy said it was like having a twin sister to add to her twin brother. Clementine hung on to Zoey's hand and insisted on sitting beside her. Andrea gave Lauren and Robert that special maternal smile that said at last everything was right in her world. Even Will, along with his wife, Olivia, and Sam and Andy and Linda and the whole Mattson clan seemed to treat her and Zoey with a special warmth. Or maybe that warmth had always been there, and she was just now letting herself feel it.

But she must listen to her doubts. Could she ever truly be a part of this wealthy family? Did she want to be? Or would her relationship with Robert somehow fail just as her marriage had?

Monday morning, before heading for his meeting with the Riverton Cattlemen's Association, Rob sat at his desk for his daily Bible reading and prayer time. As he prayed for Lauren, he remembered after church she'd seemed a little down, not like the happy lady who'd agreed to explore their relationship the night before. She and Zoey hadn't shown up for evening church, with Mandy saying Zoey had texted to say she needed to rest. Had Lauren changed her mind about him? Or did she just need a little cheering up?

He noticed the worn business card she'd given him from the Santa Fe vet sticking out from under the edge of his desk blotter. Maybe that was it. They'd never resolved the whole thing about Lady, although he'd tried to fix it last night by suggesting Zoey should train the dog. He should have apologized first and told Lauren he knew she couldn't have stolen Lady. To put a nail in the coffin of his earlier accusations, he would try again to reach that vet.

He punched in the number listed on the card. The call connected on the second ring.

"Vargas Veterinary Clinic. How may I help you?" The cheerful voice of the young woman sounded like someone who liked her job.

"May I speak to Dr. Vargas?"

"May I say who's calling?"

"Robert Mattson from the Double Bar M Ranch." Not that he needed to say that last bit. Everybody in New Mexico knew who he was. But it wouldn't hurt to add a little clout to his inquiry.

After a short pause, the woman said, "I'm sorry. Dr. Vargas is…is in surgery. Can I have him call you back?"

"Maybe you can answer my question. Do you remember last May when a lady brought in a dog she'd found and asked the doctor to check her over?"

Another pause.

"Yes. She wanted us to take the chip out of the dog's shoulder. Of course, Dr. Vargas refused, but he did give the dog they called Daisy the shots she needed. I don't know where she went after that."

Rob felt like a two-ton bull had just rammed into his chest. Barely able to speak, he managed to say, "Okay. Thanks." He disconnected the call and set his phone down.

As the numbness from the shock wore off, his first reaction was grief. Like Jordyn, Lauren had been lying all along, even dragging her sweet, innocent daughter into her deception. Anger moved in, replacing his grief. How could he have been so stupid? He'd been drawn to her beauty and sugar-sweet personality. Felt sorry for her for being a single mother with a deadbeat ex-husband and a kid to raise on her own. What a sob story. A trap that had all too easily ensnared him.

He shut his Bible and grabbed his phone and his hat. He'd have just enough time before his meeting to get to the law office and settle this once and for all. If Lauren lost her job, it was no more than she deserved. But as he sped toward town, he couldn't help but regret what would happen to Zoey once her mother was exposed as a liar and a thief.

Lauren glanced out the storefront, surprised to see Robert parking his truck and heading for the door. Her heart lifted with excitement. But instead of his usual gorgeous smile, he wore a dark frown. He burst into the reception area like an angry bear.

"Hi, Robert."

"Don't 'Hi, Robert' me, Lauren." He stood there, fists at his waist, and stared off for a moment, like he was trying to control his anger. At last, he set his fists on her desk, just like Singleton had over two weeks ago, leaning toward her in an almost threatening pose. "You lied."

"What?" She gulped down sudden fear. "What are you talking about?"

"You stole Lady and had her chip removed and—"

"Hey, Rob." Sam appeared from his back office. "What's going on?"

Robert straightened. "You should know that this woman isn't who she claims to be. She's a thief and a liar."

"Now, just a minute." Lauren stood and glared at him. "I didn't lie about finding Lady. Which you will find out if you will simply call Dr. Vargas."

"I just did." Robert huffed out a cross breath. "And you know what I found out? I found out you asked him to remove Lady's chip, but he refused."

If he'd slapped her, it couldn't hurt any more than his false accusation. "That's not true. Dr. Vargas scanned her and told me she didn't have a chip." She couldn't stop her sudden tears. "We had a big discussion about it. Surely he remembers. Why would he lie to you?"

"Because you're the one who's lying."

"Hold on a minute, Cuz." Sam touched Robert's shoulder. "Let's go back to my office so you can cool down."

"Don't bother." Lauren couldn't stay here. Not another second. Grabbing her coat and purse, she rushed out of the building and drove home. She'd been smart to listen to her doubts. Just as she'd suspected, she would never find happiness with Robert.

In the dim first-floor hallway at her apartment house, she made out a black-and-white object in front of her door.

"Lady! How did you get inside?" A helpful neighbor must have let her in after seeing her here all last summer. Lauren knelt and petted the dog, who looked past her expectantly. "No, Zoey's not here. And you shouldn't be, either." Now Robert would never believe the truth. Not that she should care what that bully thought.

She took Lady inside and gave her some water, then found the brush Zoey had used to clean her last summer. From the dirt and burrs on her coat, she'd obviously come from the ranch, as she had several weeks ago. Lauren would have to take her back right away. Except, in her state of mind, she shouldn't drive anywhere. She would just have to endure whatever cruel words Robert threw at her.

In the quiet of her apartment, she fell on her bed and wept with great, gulping sobs. A happy life with Robert had just been too much to hope for.

Lady jumped up on the bed and snuggled against her, looking into her eyes with what seemed like understanding. Lauren hugged her close. "You're such a good girl, Lady."

Tears spent, she sat on the edge of her bed and considered what to do. She'd saved a little money over these past few months, so maybe she and Zoey could go back to Orlando. Dad had said they were welcome home anytime. But taking Zoey back into Singleton's sphere of influence was too dangerous. What could she do? Where could she go?

Of course the first thing she had to do was take Lady back to the ranch. Robert's face came to mind. He'd reminded her of an angry grizzly. Well, now she was angry, too. Angry with herself for not heeding her internal warnings that he was a bully, just like Singleton. Angry that he'd wooed her with all of his cowboy charms, and she'd begun to fall for him. Today was a blessing in disguise because now she saw him as he truly was, and she wouldn't make the mistake of getting involved with the wrong man again.

But what if he had her charged with theft? Would she go to jail? What would happen to Zoey? Lauren would be forced to rely on her parents to take care of her. Then Singleton could make use of this to further his political plans and take their daughter away from her for good.

Her tears renewed, and she wept long and hard, then fell asleep, not waking up until she heard Zoey unlocking the apartment door. Lady jumped off the bed and dashed from the room. Lauren hurried to the bathroom, shut the door and tried to lessen the puffiness of her face with cold water.

"Mom?" Zoey stood outside the door. "What's Lady doing here? Why are you home this early?"

Lauren couldn't respond for the renewed tears clogging her throat.

"Mom, are you okay?"

No, I'm not okay. "Be out in a minute." Somehow she managed a cheerful tone. "Go fix yourself a snack."

What could she tell Zoey about this horrible situation? The temptation to invent a lie, to pack up her daughter and run away from Riverton and all its inhabitants, was strong. No, she had never lied to Zoey, and she wasn't about to do so now. Despite what Robert Mattson V thought, she was not a liar.

"You gonna tell me why my paralegal just ran out of the office like a scared rabbit?" Sam waved Rob to a chair beside his desk in the back office.

Rob huffed out a long breath. "Yeah, I'll be happy to." *No, not happy. Downright miserable.* "You know that story she told us about how she ended up with Lady?" At Sam's nod, he continued. "Well, it was a lie. I just called that vet clinic and learned Lauren took Lady there to get her chip removed."

"Hmm." Sam scratched his chin. "That doesn't sound right. Exactly what did the vet say?"

Count on a lawyer to want details.

"I didn't talk to the vet. His receptionist answered the phone. She remembered Lauren bringing Lady in and trying to get Dr. Vargas to—" Rob narrowed his eyes. "You look like you don't believe me."

"'Course I do, Cuz." Sam chuckled. "But I have a strange feeling about this. Lauren is painstaking in her honesty. She's saved Will and me from countless mistakes in our work. I can't see her lying about a dog."

Rob felt an odd fist of doubt grip his chest. "She's just got you fooled, like she did me."

"Fooled? I don't think so." Sam offered him a sympathetic smile, which Rob didn't appreciate. He wasn't the one in the wrong here. "I don't think you do, either. From the looks on both of your faces yesterday at church, I can see your relationship's growing pretty well. We're all real happy about that."

Rob snorted out a laugh. "Yeah, that was before I called the vet."

Sam regarded him for a full ten seconds. "Tell you what. Let me call that vet and see what I can find out."

"Sure. Here's my phone."

"No, I'll use mine. Give me the number." Sam copied the number, then put his phone on speaker.

"Vargas Veterinary Clinic. How may I help you?"

"Yeah, hey there, ma'am. Can I speak to Doc Vargas?" Sam spoke with a cowboy drawl.

"May I say who's calling?"

He paused. "Samuel Andrew."

Rob frowned. Why didn't his cousin give his last name?

"One moment, please."

After a click, a man answered. "Dr. Vargas here."

"Yessir. I wonder if you can help me. Do you remember last—" Sam glanced at Rob, one eyebrow raised in question.

"May," Rob mouthed.

"Last May," Sam continued. "A woman and her daughter brought in a dog they'd found and asked you to check for a chip so they could find her owner."

Rob's heart was in his throat. *Lord, please...* He didn't even know what to pray.

"Sure do. A sweet little black-and-white border collie with a white heart-shaped marking on her chest. Poor little dog was dehydrated and undernourished. I checked for a chip, but she didn't have one. Gave her shots and..."

"No chip?" Rob burst out. "Are you sure?"

"Look, I know how to do my job. There was an infected scar where it looked like one had been removed." The vet sounded on guard. "Who am I talking to?"

"I'm the dog's owner." Rob's pulse kicked up. "She's home with me now."

"Glad to hear it. I'd like to hear how she got there. For the record, you owe that lady and her daughter a big debt of gratitude. In another day or two on the prairie, that little dog probably would have died without them rescuing her."

Rob rocked back in his chair, for the second time today feeling like he'd been slammed in the chest by a two-ton bull. Lauren hadn't lied. She *had* saved Lady. More than that, she was every decent thing he had come to believe she was. And he'd just destroyed any chance of their relationship growing deeper.

Still on the phone, Sam launched into the story about how Lady had found her way home to the ranch. Rob grabbed his hat and waved to his cousin. "Thanks."

Now what? The memory of the fear on Lauren's face made him sick to his stomach. She'd looked that way when her ex had threatened her, and Rob had proved himself to be no better than that scumbag. How could he make it up to her? Would she ever forgive him? And if she didn't, would he ever be able to forgive himself?

Chapter Sixteen

After struggling to find words to explain the situation, Lauren couldn't come up with anything that wouldn't alarm Zoey. Maybe the less said, the better.

She went to her room, where she found Lady gazing up into Zoey's face with her usual affection.

"Come on, you two. Time to take this little rascal home."

Zoey sighed. "Yes, ma'am." She put her jacket back on. "Let's go, Lady."

Once they were on the way, Zoey said, "Mom, I don't know how we can keep her from coming to see us."

"I don't, either, honey." Right now, Lauren's main concern was how to sneak Lady onto the ranch without running into Robert. If he saw them with Lady, he might have her arrested on the spot, as he'd wanted to do that August day when they first met. Or, rather, when he'd accosted them.

Lord, You know the truth. Please protect us from Robert's anger and...and vengeance.

After she pushed the intercom button by the gate, Andrea answered.

"Lauren, what a nice surprise. Come on in."

The gate swung open, and Lauren drove toward the house. Robert's red pickup was parked near the barn. If he was down there, maybe they could avoid seeing him. Or being seen by him.

Mandy, Bobby and Clementine met them at the back door.

Along with their grandmother, they all had a good laugh over Lady's misbehavior. Despite her panicked urge to flee the premises, Lauren managed a smile.

"Yes, she's a handful. Well, we'd better get going. Zoey has homework."

"No, I don't, Mom. I finished it in study hall."

"Good," Andrea said. "You can stay for supper."

While the girls squealed their joy and Bobby grinned his approval, Lauren's heart sank again. "No, I'm afraid not. Come on, Zoey. Bobby, please hold on to Lady."

She headed out the door, practically dragging Zoey to the car. As she was about to climb in, she saw Robert striding toward her across the barnyard like Marshal Dillon coming to arrest a cattle rustler. Hands shaking, she managed to get the key in the ignition, start the car and drive quickly toward the gate, gravel flying from beneath her wheels and her heart pounding in her chest.

"Look out!" The panic in Zoey's voice brought her to her senses.

She managed to stop before reaching the busy highway, where a huge semi tractor-trailer truck roared past them. If she hadn't stopped, the truck would have hit them. Her heart raced.

"Mom, what's wrong?"

"Nothing, sweetheart." Well, there she went, telling a lie to her precious daughter after all. But what else could she have said?

Rob didn't blame Lauren for hightailing it off the ranch property. He must have scared her bad, when all he wanted to do was take her in his arms and beg her forgiveness. Now he'd have to wait to tell her how wrong he'd been. No, it was worse than just being wrong. He'd believed the lies of a stranger rather than believing the good he saw in her with his own eyes. Worse still, he'd laid on her the blame for Jordyn's deceptions. But he'd already forgiven Jordyn and asked the Lord to forgive him for his failures as a husband. With Lauren, there was nothing to forgive. The only thing she'd stolen was his heart, and now he'd deeply wounded hers by believing a lie.

Sam had called this afternoon and reported the rest of his conversation with Dr. Vargas. Seemed the receptionist had been mistaken about the chip, although when Rob talked to the girl, she'd been adamant about remembering Lauren's visit to the clinic. Even remembered they'd called his dog Daisy. Why would a stranger in a responsible position at a veterinary clinic lie like that about someone she'd just met?

That would have to remain a mystery, but Rob no longer cared about that young woman's motivation. He only wanted a chance to make things right with Lauren, to possibly gain her forgiveness. His guilt only compounded when he found the family gathered around their wayward border collie. Once again, Lauren had proved herself to be honorable. A thief would have done her best to hide Lady to repay him for accosting her this morning. Rob hadn't told Mom about that disaster, so he did his best to act like everything was okay. But when Mom said Lauren had turned down her invitation to supper, it struck another blow. Of course she wouldn't want to face him, because she didn't know he'd finally learned the truth—the real truth—from the vet. So what was a chump cowboy to do to regain his lady's trust?

After the kids went to bed, Mom casually mentioned something about flowers. Had her radar picked up the signal that all was not well between him and Lauren?

Sam hadn't offered any advice on how to fix the situation, but what did his young bachelor cousin know about relationships when he rarely even dated? One thing was sure. If Rob approached Lauren, he'd better take flowers—as Mom had slyly suggested—along with a large helping of humble pie, and not stride toward her like a lawman out to arrest an outlaw. He had some time-consuming work to do on the ranch that couldn't wait, so he'd give her time to cool down and see her at Bible study on Wednesday evening.

Except she didn't show up at the church that evening. As worry ate a hole in his chest, Rob couldn't concentrate on the lesson. After the final prayer, he beat a hasty retreat before anybody could question him about Lauren's absence. What could he say? What could he do?

Mom's idea of flowers came to mind. That was it. First thing tomorrow, he'd go to Cousin Jenny's florist shop and buy every red rose she had, then head over to the law office. But Jenny had only a half dozen red roses, not enough to show Lauren how serious he was. While he waited, Jenny called her supplier in Albuquerque, who promised to ship them right away, but they wouldn't arrive until tomorrow, Friday. Rob hated to wait another day, but, coward that he was, he needed those flowers for a shield when he went to see Lauren.

The next day, he took a two-dozen red rose bouquet, all fancied up with greenery and little white flowers, and made his way through town to the law office. To his disappointment, Lauren was not at her desk, and no coat hung on the rack in the corner.

"Hey, Rob." Will came out to greet him. "Wow, those are beautiful roses. Um, I assume they're for Lauren, right?"

Rob had never liked humbling himself before his younger cousins. After all, he'd always been like a big brother to these two guys, someone they'd always looked up to. But right now he had no cause for pride. "Yeah. Is she coming in? I sort of owe her an apology."

"You sure do." Sam joined them. "Those flowers might just get you a hearing, even though you don't deserve it."

"Thanks a lot." Rob exhaled crossly. "Did you tell her about our phone call to the vet?"

Sam held up both hands and backed away. "No way. That's

between you and Lauren. I learned long ago not to involve myself in lovers' quarrels."

"Thanks for nothing." Rob scowled at him. "All right, then. When will she be in?"

"Don't you remember?" Will gave him an odd look. "This is the weekend Zoey's competing in the computer programming contest in Albuquerque. They won't be back until late Saturday."

Rob stared at his cousins for several moments, not at all helped by their amused smiles. Didn't they know how serious this was? Finally, he thrust the flowers at Will. "Here. Give these to Olivia. If you don't owe her an apology now, you will one day." He strode out of the building to the sound of their laughter. But for Rob, this was anything but funny.

That evening, he ate pizza with Bobby's football team, Coach Johnson's attempt to cheer them up after losing their final home game of the season. As a second stringer, Bobby hadn't played, of course, but he didn't look as dejected as the other boys on the team. Probably because his heart had never been in the game. Lauren had been right. Bobby should have gone to the programming meet where, with Zoey's help, he would be on the team's first string.

Lauren hated driving in the dark, but they'd had supper in Albuquerque before the drive home. Zoey rode in the front passenger seat of their little Honda and chatted over her shoulder with her teammates, Grace Martinez and Jeff Sizemore, about the success of their strategies in the competition. They'd done pretty well for sophomores against some more experienced teams and were now making plans for the spring programming meet. Their coach and the other team of three Riverton students followed in a pickup behind her car.

Occasionally, Lauren caught a hint of ridicule in Jeff's voice mimicking Zoey's pronunciations and the way she often had to push her words out on a hum. Lauren hadn't been around the boy long enough to know whether he was teasing or being mean. She had to trust Zoey to choose her friends, but if the boy wore down her daughter's hard-won self-confidence, Lauren might have to turn Mama Bear and have a word with him.

They arrived at Jeff's house around ten o'clock, and she helped him sort his bag out from the pile in the back of the car. From inside the small wood frame house came yelling, at least one barking dog and a few loud thumps.

"Jeff, do you want me to help—"

"No!" He grabbed his backpack. "I don't need nothing from you." He trudged away across the patchy, unkempt yard, shoulders slumped, like a reluctant soldier going into battle.

Poor kid. His homelife must be difficult. No wonder he'd begged Coach Smith to let him fill in for Bobby on the team, even though his poor grades in other classes should have disqualified him.

After taking Grace home, Lauren drove to their apartment. She and Zoey were both exhausted from their busy two days. Should they go to church tomorrow or stay home and rest? Zoey answered that without a word when she woke up Sunday morning with a headache. Although Lauren would never wish her daughter to have any pain or illness, and although neither one of them wanted to miss church, she was more than glad not to have to face Robert and his accusations. Or watch his friends side with him and write her off as a dog thief.

At least Sam and Will hadn't fired her. Which seemed a little strange after the scene Robert created last Monday. In fact, on Tuesday when she'd returned to work, Sam hadn't even mentioned it. She didn't know whether to be grateful or fearful that the ax might yet fall any day now, and she sure wouldn't bring it up.

After a day of rest, Zoey felt well enough to go to school on Monday. "Mom, are we going to the ranch for my riding lesson on Saturday?" The worry in her voice told Lauren she'd picked up on her broken relationship with Robert. Since he hadn't made a move to arrest her and her bosses were surprisingly quiet about the scene he'd caused, Lauren decided she would risk it for Zoey's sake.

"Sure. Pretty soon it'll be too cold for riding, and I know you appreciate the exercise."

What was the worst that could happen? No, better not try to guess.

On Friday, seated in a hard chair in the final meeting of the state cattlemen's association, Rob fidgeted and resisted the urge to check the time on his Apple Watch…again. Thoughts of Lauren had dominated his mind this past week, but he'd been stuck here in Santa Fe, tending to his responsibilities to the ranch and to the larger cattle raising community. As president of the local cattlemen's association, he'd come to the capital to present to the legislative committee a new proposal for controlling river pollution. Before that, he'd had to put out some fires with the Riverton Stampede Committee because the provider for the livestock had backed out due to overcommitment to other rodeos. While these were important affairs he enjoyed managing, nothing would be right in his world until he settled things with Lauren. After his rotten, unfounded accusations, if she never spoke to him again, it was no more than he deserved.

When she hadn't shown up for church last Sunday, he should have just gone to her apartment and made his apology, even without flowers, but decided it was better not to intrude if Zoey wasn't feeling well. Now he'd been stuck here in Santa Fe since Monday, unable to solve the problem hammering at his heart and soul and starting a heartburn fire no over-the-counter medication could put out.

Once the meeting was dismissed, he declined invitations

to lunch and headed back to Riverton. Ten miles down the road, he made a U-turn. Time to find out why that receptionist lied to him about Lauren. He took the tattered business card from his wallet and punched the address of Vargas Veterinary Clinic into his navigation system, then drove there. And took a few minutes to quiet his temper before entering the building.

Inside he approached the reception desk, where a dark-haired, middle-aged lady sat at a computer.

"May I help you?"

With her deep alto voice and Hispanic inflections, she clearly was not the woman he'd talked to when he and Sam called here last week.

"Yes, ma'am." He glanced at her name tag. "Howdy, Miz Vargas. Last May a friend of mine—" if only he could still claim that relationship with Lauren "—brought in my lost border collie for a checkup. She'd found the dog beside the road, and she was pretty thin. I wanted to drop by and thank Dr. Vargas in person for taking such good care of Lady...Daisy."

The woman's face blossomed into a smile. "Oh, that's so kind of you. My husband will be happy to hear that." She punched an intercom. "*Querido*, can you come out here a minute?"

While they waited for him, Rob looked around the reception area, where several people sat with their cats, birds and other critters in small cages.

"It must be nice to work with your husband." Rob considered his next words carefully. "Was that your daughter who was working here when my friend brought Daisy in?"

"That one? Humph. Juliet Sizemore is no daughter of mine." Mrs. Vargas scowled. "She was trouble from the start. My husband is a kind man, but even he had enough of her giving out diagnoses over the phone, sometimes outright telling lies to people. He let her go last week."

"Juliet Sizemore, eh?" Rob blew out a long breath. That explained everything. If memory served him, and it did in this case, Juliet was Jeff's older sister. That troubled family caused nothing but grief for themselves and everybody who knew them. Once he told her his name, she probably figured she could create mischief by lying about Lauren. And she sure had.

Dr. Vargas emerged from the back hallway, and Rob shook his hand and thanked him for contributing to "Daisy's" return to health. After several moments of friendly chatter about the animals they both worked with, Rob took his leave. Tomorrow was Saturday. Would Lauren bring Zoey out to the ranch for a lesson? And would she give him a chance to apologize? To repair the damage he'd done to their growing relationship, maybe even shattering it forever?

With fifteen years of practice, Lauren managed to keep her emotions subdued in front of Zoey as they drove out to the ranch on Saturday morning. She parked in her regular spot by the picket fence gate near the big house and walked across the barnyard with her daughter. Lady raced from the barn to greet Zoey, and after receiving the necessary hug, walked beside her the rest of the way. Mandy, Bobby and Clementine awaited them, along with shovels and wheelbarrow ready for the usual mucking of the stalls. As always, laughter and teasing filled the air. And, as always, Lauren watched in amazement while they did a chore most people would consider disgusting. Obviously the love of horses and riding made it, if not a pleasure, a necessity worth doing for the reward upon its completion.

While she hovered near in case Zoey needed help in saddling Tripper, she felt Robert's presence before she saw him emerge from the back of the barn, leading a saddled horse.

"Hey." He had the nerve to smile at her, as if their last encounter less than two weeks ago hadn't been the second worst event in her entire life.

"Hi." She moved closer to Tripper's head and held the bridle while Bobby helped Zoey lift the blanket and saddle to the horse's back. Lady was in the middle of it all, as though she was making sure Zoey was okay.

"I'm glad you came." Robert paused several yards away.

She slid him a doubtful look.

"I wanted to tell you—"

"Daddy, can I ride with you today? Pleeease?" Little Clementine's pleading stirred Lauren's heart. It also cut off whatever Robert started to say, for which Lauren was grateful.

He blew out a breath. "No, kiddo. I've already told you you're not ready to ride out with the big kids."

Tears streaming down her cheeks, Clementine ran from the barn. While the twins didn't appear to notice, Zoey did. She knelt beside Lady. "Go play with Clementine. I'm gonna ride Tripper now."

Instead of obeying, Lady grabbed the hem of Zoey's jeans and tugged.

"No, Lady. Don't do that." Zoey tried to retrieve her pant leg, but Lady held on tight and even growled softly. "No, Lady, not now. I'm gonna ride. We can play later." She looked at Lauren. "Mom, will you hold her?"

"Sure." Lauren gripped Lady's collar, and the dog whined. "As soon as you're up on the horses, we'll go find Clementine."

Her heart aching for the little girl, Lauren looked over to see Robert staring at her, but in the shadowed aisle couldn't make out his expression. Why didn't he go ahead and say whatever Clementine had interrupted? Maybe he decided this wasn't the time to air the unpleasantness between them.

He stepped closer. "I thought I'd take the kids down by the river, if that's okay with you. When we come back, I want to talk to you." His whispered words had often given her pleasant shivers, but this time, the shivers held a foreboding.

"No, thank you. You've already told me everything I need to know."

Sudden tears slipped down her cheeks, so she held on to Lady's collar and walked from the barn to keep the kids from noticing. And Robert, of course. She strolled toward her car to wait for Zoey, and noticed on her left the pretty adobe house he'd offered to her so Zoey could live here and train Lady. That he would give up his idea about Bobby training the dog showed he was willing to change his mind about important matters. Now if only he would change his mind about her. That wasn't likely to happen. After his horrible accusations, did she even want it to?

Once he and the kids rode out of the barn, down the hill and out of sight, she let Lady go. "Go find Clementine, Lady. That's a good girl."

Lady sniffed the air, as if undecided which way to go. Finally, she scampered away, so Lauren settled in the front passenger seat of her car, hoping Andrea wouldn't look outside and notice her. No doubt Robert had told his mother about accosting Lauren, and of course she would take her son's side, just as Lauren's parents had always believed Singleton's versions of their conflicts. For now, she would try to enjoy this beautiful though chilly day, knowing at least Zoey was having a good time. Cattle mooing in the front pasture had become familiar to her. She would miss that soothing sound when she and Zoey no longer came out to the ranch.

Rob followed the kids as they rode beyond the levee to the trail down by the river. The flow of water had slowed since summer, so they had a smooth, solid path for easy riding. As much as he wanted to enjoy this time with the kids while he planned a way to apologize to Lauren, he kept thinking about Lady's odd behavior in grabbing Zoey's pant leg. Was she just playing or—

"Dad, look!" Mandy pointed toward a calf entangled in tree branches and river debris.

Before Rob could grab the rope from his saddle horn, Mandy already had her lasso in hand. With skill he didn't know she possessed, she lassoed the maverick and, with a quick command to her horse to stand, jumped from the saddle to free the calf. Rob could only watch in amazement. When had his young daughter developed a calf-roping skill worthy of a grown-up cowboy in rodeo competition?

"Good job, Mandy." Bobby dismounted and ran to help. He whipped out his pocketknife and began cutting away at the smaller branches entangling the calf.

"Wow, you guys are amazing." Zoey sounded a little tired. "I wish—"

Rob watched in horror as her eyes closed, and she rocked to the side. He spurred his horse up close and put an arm around her waist, just as her head lolled back.

"Lord, help me. Bobby, grab Tripper's bridle." He gently tugged Zoey from the saddle onto his own horse and cradled her in his arms. "You two take care of the maverick. Get him back up to his mama. And bring Tripper. I'm taking Zoey to the house."

Riding slowly back up the trail and over the levee, he now understood Lady's actions. She'd sensed that Zoey was about to have a seizure and didn't want her to ride. What an incredible dog. Maybe…no, he couldn't think beyond taking care of this precious girl he'd come to love almost as much as he loved his own kids.

Lulled by the sun's mild warmth, Lauren dozed off, until a distant shriek sounded from the front pasture. Clementine! She shook off her stupor and hurried across the barnyard. Another shriek sent her into a run. Inside the fenced pasture, the crying little girl sat on the ground all too near the milling cattle. Lady barked at them, herding them away to the other side.

Lauren had always avoided getting close to these big animals, but she pushed away her fear and opened the gate and ran to Clementine.

"What happened, honey?"

"I tripped on that." She pointed at the offending rock. "And hurt my leg. Oww!" Her loud sobs broke Lauren's heart.

Several of the steers, possibly stirred up by her noisy wailing, milled around nervously, with Lady continuing to bark and drive them back.

Lauren gently touched Clementine's leg, which brought on another scream. Again the cattle moved closer. Lauren needed to get her out of here.

"Honey, I'm going to pick you up. Hold on to my neck."

She managed to lift her and stagger toward the gate. The child laid her head against Lauren's upper arm, sobbing. Maternal love and protectiveness surged through her chest. "You're going to be okay, sweetheart." She managed to close and lock the gate behind them.

Lady trotted along beside them, casting anxious looks at Clementine.

To Lauren's surprise, Robert's horse was tied to the fence near the gate, and he was hurrying toward the back door with Zoey in his arms. Lady darted ahead to join them.

"Zoey!" Alarm for her own daughter gripped her, but she held on to Clementine even tighter.

"Robert, what happened?" Had Zoey fallen off of Tripper? Or—

He paused, trying to open the back door. "She—"

"I'm okay, Mom." Zoey looked weary, as she always did after a seizure. "You can put me down, Mr. Mattson."

"When we get inside—" He turned toward Lauren, and his eyes widened. "Clementine! What happened?" His tone sounded accusing.

Did he think his daughter's accident was Lauren's fault? What else would he blame her for?

"Daddy, I wanted to get Lady to herd the cows. I thought if I did, you'd be happy with me. Ow!" she cried again. Lady gave her an anxious look.

"Honey, I'm happy with you." His voice broke in a tone of tender regret Lauren hadn't heard before. "I love you, punkin." He glanced at Lauren. "Let's get these two inside."

His quick cooling of his anger surprised her. Maybe he'd just been upset when he saw Clementine in her arms.

As they settled their girls on the couches in the great room, Lady glanced between them as though trying to decide which one needed her most. She sat beside Zoey, as did Lauren.

Robert pulled out his cell phone and punched it.

"I'm okay, Mom." Zoey gave Lauren a sad smile. "Just a little weak. I forgot to take my Keppra this morning."

Lauren brushed a hand across her cheek. "Oh, honey, I should have checked to be sure you did. I think we need to have the doctor check you."

"Oh, my poor baby." Andrea sat beside Clementine and gently removed her sneaker, which caused more wailing.

"We'll be there in ten minutes." Robert disconnected his call. "Mom, can you make sure the twins are okay? They're coming up from the river. I'm taking Clementine to the ER." He looked at Lauren. "And Zoey?" At least this time he asked instead of telling her what he planned.

"I'll take her."

He sighed. "Lauren, please go with me. I need you to hold Clementine while I drive."

"I—I…wouldn't she prefer her grandmother?"

"I need Mom to help the kids with the horses." He gave her another pained look. "Please. Maybe Zoey can lie down in the back seat?" He glanced at Zoey.

She gave him a weak smile. "I can do that."

"Okay. Sure." Lauren bit her lip.

During the trip to town, the silence in the truck was broken only by Clementine's hiccuping sobs. Careful of her injury, Lauren held her close, treasuring the feel of the sweet child in her arms and wishing it were under very different circumstances. At the ER, the orthopedic specialist took charge of Clementine, and Doc Edwards checked Zoey's vital signs. Once he'd cleared her daughter, Lauren eyed the door, eager to leave, but her car and even her purse were still at the ranch.

X-rays completed, pain shots administered, the orthopedist proclaimed only a hairline break above Clementine's ankle and, with his nurse's assistance, proceeded to apply padding and a plaster cast. With the painkiller taking effect, Clementine giggled as the doctor made jokes and silly faces. She also demanded that Lauren should still hold her hand during the process. Zoey sat in a chair, her color returning by the minute. Robert watched from the corner where he leaned against the wall, arms crossed.

"Can I get you some coffee?" His question surprised her.

"From the machine?"

"That's the only kind available on the weekend." From his slight grin, maybe he was remembering their previous coffee disaster when Zoey had been here the first time. She'd enjoyed their joking about the undrinkable brew.

"Ugh." She grimaced. "No, thanks."

He chuckled. Oh, how she had missed that sound.

What was she thinking? This man had accused her of stealing and lying. Now he was all nice and *Please help me*? No thanks to the coffee *and* to him.

On the way home, Clementine fell asleep in her arms, and Zoey dozed in the back seat. Again, Lauren's maternal instincts kicked in. She'd loved being a mother from the moment she'd discovered her pregnancy. Had loved Zoey through every childhood illness and accident and especially her triumphs over her CP challenges. She would have loved having another child or two, but it hadn't been the Lord's will for her. Just as marital happiness had eluded her.

Halfway back to the ranch, Robert interrupted her musings. "Thanks for your help."

"No problem." Not that she'd had a choice, but she was glad she'd come to help with Clementine. To avoid looking at him, she stared out the passenger side window.

"It's good that Zoey's resting."

"Uh-huh."

He must have taken the hint because he quit trying to engage her in conversation. At the house, Robert carried still-sleeping Clementine, and Lauren helped Zoey inside. Andrea and the twins gathered around to be sure both girls were all right. Lady nuzzled Zoey's hand, then sniffed Clementine's cast and looked into the child's face, her sweet way of checking on her humans.

"Is Clementine's leg broken?" Mandy asked.

"Can we sign her cast?" Bobby grabbed a Sharpie from a side table drawer.

"Shh," Robert said. "Let's let her sleep." He looked at Lauren. "Will you wait while I get her settled? I want…need to talk to you."

"No, Zoey needs to rest, and I have laundry to do." Lauren beckoned to her daughter. "Come on, honey. Bobby, please hold Lady so she won't follow us."

Even though Zoey was tired during the drive home, she talked about her ride by the river. "Mom, I wish you could have seen Mandy lasso the stray calf. She was awesome."

"That *is* awesome." If only Robert would admit his older daughter was a true cowgirl.

"I'm not afraid to ride again." Zoey laughed softly. "But I'll listen to Lady next time. And I'll make sure I take my meds."

Lauren sent her a rueful smile. "We'll see."

Her daughter was brave. Lauren, not so much. She couldn't

escape the thought that she'd been a coward for running away rather than having a final confrontation with Robert. Why not deal with it once and for all?

Easy answer. Her heart was still broken from his unfounded accusations, and she couldn't bear to face any further censure.

Chapter Seventeen

Mom pulled back the covers so Rob could lay Clementine in her bed. Once settled, she looked at peace and oh so sweet. Doc said she'd experience some pain once the painkillers wore off. Rob sat on the chair beside her bed, intending to be there for her when she woke up to make sure she understood how much he loved her. It cut real deep that she'd preferred Lauren's support while the doctor applied the cast. What hurt worse was she thought she had to earn his love. Had he been that neglectful of his youngest? It sickened him to think she'd entered a pasture with a herd of unruly yearling cattle and could easily have been trampled. If not for Lady's protection and Lauren's quick action, she might have been.

He'd been wrong about Lauren. Neglectful of Clementine. Totally missed the mark with Mandy. Man, who would have thought she could lasso a struggling calf on the first throw? What other ranch chores did she do well? Yes, Bobby could do it all, however reluctantly. But he'd been a bench warmer on a losing football squad when he could have earned some points on the school programming team if Rob hadn't been so stubborn about his activities.

"Daddy, where's Miss Lauren?" Clementine rubbed her eyes, only half-awake.

"Hey, sweetheart. She and Zoey had to go home." To do

her laundry, her overused excuse for escaping his company. "But here's Lady."

Lady put her paws on the edge of the bed and touched her nose to Clementine's hand. Clementine petted her. "You saved me, Lady."

"Punkin, you know I love you, don't you?" He brushed her hair back from her face.

"Uh-huh. I love you, too." She gave him a teary smile, then drifted off to sleep again.

"Robert, I can watch over her now." Mom touched his shoulder. "I don't know what happened between you and Lauren, but why not go after her and settle it? Don't let the sun go down on your wrath."

His wrath? That was the whole problem summed up in one short scripture verse. He'd wanted to deepen his relationship with Lauren, but had all too easily believed some stranger's lie. In truth, Lauren had rescued Clementine and showered her with tender care, just as she did her own child. She was everything he could hope for in…in what? Friendship? Relationship? Wife? Had he been using fear as a shield not to love her when all the while his heart was telling him something different? He'd finally gotten around to reading Zoey's essay about how they found Lady, and it had doubled his grief over his terrible treatment of Lauren. She'd been telling the truth all along.

"Thanks, Mom." He grunted. "I have more than one fire to put out tonight."

He made his way to Mandy's room and stuck his head in. She was bent over her homework. "Hey, cowgirl, that was some pretty fancy roping this afternoon."

"Thanks, Dad." She grinned at his praise.

"Yeah, I've been thinking. If you want, you can help with calving in the spring. What would you think about that?"

Her grinned broadened. "I'd love it!"

"Good. Maybe we can put you to work on more of the ranch chores. You up for that?"

"Yessir." Her eyes filled with tears, the happy kind. "I won't let you down, Dad."

"I know you won't, honey. Now get that homework done." He turned from the doorway before she saw his own eyes tearing up. Next problem to solve, Bobby. He went to the room across the hall from Mandy's.

Bobby sat on his bed, propped up on pillows, his computer resting on his knees and a headset covering his ears.

"Hey, kiddo." Rob walked over and glanced at the laptop. The screen showed some complicated coding way beyond Rob's comprehension. He removed Bobby's headset. The boy blinked in his preoccupied way.

"Oh, hey, Dad."

"Hey." Rob sat on the edge of the bed. "Looks like you're working on some interesting stuff."

"Yessir." Bobby's expression grew guarded. "I'm not goofing off. It's homework."

"Sure. I believe you." Now the tough part. "Look, I've been thinking maybe you should spend more time with the programming team. That's where your talents seem to lie. What would you think of that?"

"You mean it?" Bobby grew animated. "What about football?"

"Well, you still have two years to go." This was the hardest for Rob to let go of. "If you still feel the same way next fall, you...you don't have to play."

"Wow." Bobby gave him his goofy grin. "Thanks, Dad. I won't let you down."

That's what Mandy had said. Had he been such an exacting dad to these two? That needed to end. Today. "I know you won't, son."

With one more score to settle, he told Mom he was leaving.

The sun was nearing the horizon, and as she'd said, he wasn't going to let it go down until matters were settled with Lauren. He'd planned to buy more flowers to use as a shield when he apologized, but Jenny's shop would be closed by now, and he couldn't delay this any longer. He stood by the pickup for a moment. "Lord, what can I do to show her how sorry I am for being a beast? For believing the worst about her?"

He knew the answer right away and went back into the house to fetch the only gift that would solve this problem once and for all.

As much as Lauren had often longed for a happy, stable marriage, she'd learned over the years such happiness wasn't meant for her. Then Robert came into her life...rather, *barged* into her life, and she'd begun to dream again.

What should she do now? Today he seemed to have softened toward her, probably because they were with the kids. Could she trust him not to blow up at her again? At least her job was safe. Probably. Over the past week, Sam and Will had left subtle hints about how much they depended on her, and on Friday, proved it outright by giving her a significant raise in salary. Now she could buy Zoey some much-needed winter clothes.

Robert had let Zoey ride today, had saved her from falling off Tripper when she had her seizure. He'd been so gentle to dear little Clementine, proving he truly was a loving father. Indeed, he was kind and caring...to everyone but her.

Zoey had taken a short nap and now sat in the living room folding laundry, so Lauren started supper. Hands deep in chopping salad greens, she grabbed a carrot stick to nibble, which only made her stomach rumble with hunger. A tasty steak came to mind, but she couldn't afford that luxury.

A knock sounded on the door, reverberating throughout the small apartment.

"I'll get it." Zoey walked across the room, her broken gait showing her weariness from the day. "Lady!"

"What?" Lauren dried her hands and walked to the living room. Her heart seemed to stop. "Robert."

Zoey was down on her knees receiving wet doggy kisses and laughing. "Did you come for a visit, silly girl?"

"No." Robert gazed at Lauren as he answered. "She's come to stay."

"Now, just a minute—" Heat rushed up Lauren's neck, but she tried to tamp down her anger.

"I mean, would you please take care of my, *this* dog, who clearly wants to be with Zoey?" He shuffled his feet in true shy cowboy fashion. "Lauren, I'm sorry for—"

"Zoey, take Lady to your room and close the door."

Zoey looked between her and Robert and grinned. "Yes, ma'am." She quickly obeyed.

Lauren fisted her hands at her waist. "Now, what's this all about?"

He took a step toward her. She held up her hands palms out to stop him, then crossed her arms.

"I'm so sorry for not trusting you. I was so wrong to believe that woman at the vet clinic. She told me you asked Dr. Vargas to remove Lady's chip, but he refused to do it. But when I called back, I mean, when *Sam* called back, the doctor himself said there was no chip and that you and Zoey saved Lady's life."

That was a big speech for this cowboy, and the sorrow in his face, in his entire demeanor, backed up his words.

"Please forgive me, Lauren. I don't deserve it, but—"

"Do you have any idea how much you hurt me? How you, a prominent citizen of this county, this *state*, cast aspersions on my character? I work in a law office. How would it look to clients who trust your cousins if their paralegal isn't honest?"

"I know." He nodded, and his eyes reddened. "If it's any

help, my cousins were smarter than me. Like I said, Sam followed up my call with one of his own. He didn't give his last name to the woman who answered, so she had no way to connect us. Turns out she's related to the Sizemore family. They've caused trouble for the Mattsons since the late 1800s. When I gave her my name, she must have decided to cause more trouble." He seemed to realize he was still wearing his hat, because he took it off and turned it in his hands, a gesture she would have found charming once upon a time. "Is there any way I can fix this? I mean, between you and me? Lauren, I love you, and I'll do whatever it takes to make it right."

He loved her? Her eyes burned, and she took a deep breath, trying not to cry. It was no use. She burst into tears and turned away from him. She felt his big, calloused hands gently touch her shoulders. A pleasant shiver swept down her entire being.

"Lauren." He spoke her name so softly, so lovingly. "I love you," he repeated. "Please forgive me. Please tell me what I can do to make things right between us."

She turned around and gazed up into those gorgeous blue eyes. "I think you just did." She tilted her head toward Zoey's closed door. "Bringing Lady to visit Zoey means more to me than you can imagine."

"Not just bringing her for a visit. I meant what I said. I'm giving her to Zoey to keep." He brushed tears from her cheek and gently pulled her into his arms. For several moments, they gazed at each other. Lauren could hardly breathe.

"I love you," he said again.

As warmth flooded her heart, she sighed. "I love you, too, Robert."

"Oh, go ahead and kiss her, Mr. Mattson." Zoey's sudden appearance startled them from their daze. "You have my permission."

"Zoey." Robert sent her a playful scowl. "Don't you have some laundry to do?"

* * *

"So, James, how's my mother's condo coming along?" Rob stood in the great room with Mom's contractor...and whatever else he was to her. "Did you get those problems with the plumbing ironed out?"

"Yep." Dressed in jeans, boots and a checkered flannel shirt, the graying man in his sixties looked more like a cowboy than a big-city businessman. "We had to switch companies to get the job done to Andrea's satisfaction."

That usually meant more money. How did Rob go about making sure this dude wasn't bilking her out of her savings? "How much did the change cost?"

James chuckled. "Not a dime. In fact, we got a full refund and applied it to the new fixtures."

"Huh." While Rob considered what his next question should be, he glanced through the archway into the kitchen.

Lauren and Linda were helping Mom put the finishing touches on the Thanksgiving dinner. The kids were playing UNO at the kitchen table, with Lady lying on the floor between Zoey and Clementine. The aromas of roasted turkey, spicy crown roast beef and apple and pumpkin pies filled the house.

"Rob, I'm glad we have a chance to talk. I know you probably have a lot of questions." James looked directly into Rob's eyes, as he had when they met earlier and he gave Rob a firm handshake, both signs of an honest man. "I want you to know Andrea is very special to me, and I'd like to spend the rest of my life with her." He glanced toward the kitchen. "I can show you my financials, if you want. We plan to set up separate accounts so her grandkids will inherit from her, and mine will inherit from me." He inhaled a deep breath as though gathering courage. "So, if that settles the concerns any dutiful son should have, I'm asking your permission to propose to her."

With a proposal of his own in mind, Rob could feel the

small box in his jeans pocket. He still hadn't figured out how to get Lauren away from the crowd. When he'd called her dad back in Orlando and asked to marry her, Dan had been surprised. Said nobody did that anymore, but he was fine with whatever Lauren wanted to do. Not the best beginning for their relationship. No wonder Lauren often doubted herself. Rob would make sure he did better by Mom…and James.

He stuck out his hand. "I'm happy to say yes, you have my permission." As they shook hands again, he added, "Welcome to the family."

He prayed his proposal to Lauren went just as well.

Sam and Andy came in from doing chores, and everyone gathered around the table. James offered a prayer of thanks that further encouraged Rob about his spiritual condition. Conversation flowed around the table along with the food. Toward the end of the meal, with desserts calling their names, James stood up.

"Folks, I appreciate your kind hospitality. Now, if you'll indulge me, I'm about to ask Miss Andrea to be my wife—"

Laughing along with everyone else, Mom stood up beside him, clearly not surprised. "Yes!"

"Hold on a minute, honey. Let me ask you." James took a little box from his shirt and opened it to reveal a shiny, pricey sapphire-and-diamond ring. "Not gonna make a big speech, just gonna say I love you, Andrea. Will you marry me?"

Mom answered by planting a kiss on his lips. While Bobby groaned and everybody else cheered, Rob felt a small jab in his chest, but quickly dismissed it. He knew Dad would be pleased that Mom had found a good man to spend her senior years with.

Mom turned to him. "Robert, don't you have something to say to Lauren?"

"Now, Mom." He wanted to do this in private, but that maverick just broke loose. No herding it back into the corral.

"All right, then. Lauren, honey, I'm crazy about you. Will you marry me?" Ugh! He'd meant to say something flowery. Too late now. He pulled out the ring he'd chosen from among the many family heirloom jewels, Great-Grandma Mattson's legacy engagement ring, a large ruby set in gold and surrounded by emerald-cut diamonds.

"Sure. Why not?" She winked as she stood and stuck out her left hand. "Oh, Robert, it's gorgeous. Yes, I'll marry you." Once he put the ring on her finger, she cuddled up under his arm and looked up at him with those beautiful gray-green eyes.

He glanced around the table. "Y'all excuse us a minute." Then he planted a kiss on her sweet lips that lasted longer than he could count. He couldn't be sure, but he thought he heard a few more cheers and plenty of laughter from the people who loved them best.

Lauren hesitated to open personal mail at work, especially a letter bearing the return address of an Orlando law office. But, not able to concentrate on the document on her computer, she opened the ivory envelope and pulled out the letter. As she'd suspected, it was from Singleton's lawyer claiming she had pressured him into signing away his parental rights and demanding that she must grant him immediate and open visitation with Zoey. In the midst of planning her December 19 wedding, she just couldn't deal with this now. That didn't keep her from shedding a few tears.

"Hey, Lauren, what's wrong?"

Count on Sam to always be sensitive to her feelings. She handed him the letter. "What can we do?"

He grunted. "This guy just doesn't quit, does he?" He scratched his chin thoughtfully. "The easiest solution would be for you and Rob to get married right away. You've already got your wedding license, right?" At her nod, he said, "Good. Once you say 'I do' we can finish Rob's adoption petition and

have Judge Mathis sign it so Zoey's last name will be Mattson. The judge is already on our side about this because your
ex signed away his rights in Florida, and we can prove you
didn't pressure him. Besides, under New Mexico law, deadbeat
fathers can't renege on their parental responsibilities. Also, if
you want, we can get a restraining order so Parker won't be
able to approach Zoey without getting arrested. This should
be easy-peasy."

And so, two days later, Lauren found herself standing beside Robert in the Riverton Community Church sanctuary in
front of Pastor Tim, with Zoey and the kids…and Lady…as
their supporting posse. They would still have their planned
December 19 reception here at the church so all their friends
and many, many relatives could enjoy the festivities. But now
Zoey was safe with her new dad, one who wanted to be a true
father to her, not use her as a political pawn.

After the brief ceremony, the new family piled back into
Robert's pickup and headed toward the courthouse, where they
met Sam at Judge Mathis's office. With all the proper paperwork signed and sealed, they hit the road again, first stopping
at the steak house for lunch, then back in the truck, with the
kids singing silly camp songs. When Lady tired of the noise,
she lifted her voice in plaintive howls that somehow added
harmony as they drove home toward the Double Bar M Ranch.

Home. That sounded so good. Lauren could hardly wait to
begin her new life as Mrs. Robert Mattson.

Rob chuckled at the noise the kids and Lady were making. It was sweet music to him. They pulled into the barnyard,
and he parked near the picket fence. The kids hopped out of
the truck and raced toward the house, with Lady right behind
them. Rob took a little longer helping Lauren from the vehicle. He pulled her into a hug for a sweet kiss before sweeping
her up in his arms.

She squealed in surprise and laughed. "What are you doing?"

"Gotta carry my new bride over the threshold, right?"

She laughed again. "I guess you do."

He felt a paw on his jeans and looked down to see Lady eyeing them both with concern.

"It's okay, girl. Go find Zoey."

Lady tilted her head.

Lauren looked down. "It's okay, Lady. Go find Clementine."

As the dog raced off to obey them both, they shared a laugh.

"I hope she doesn't get confused," Lauren said.

"She'll get it sorted out." Of that, Rob was certain.

Lady was back home, back where she belonged. But with a new job—taking care of Rob's youngest kiddo, Clementine, and his much loved new daughter, Zoey. And all was right in his world.

* * * * *

If you enjoyed this book, be sure to look for
another K-9 Companions tale next month,
The Veteran's Valentine Helper *by Lee Tobin McClain,*
available wherever Love Inspired books are sold!

Dear Reader,

Thank you for choosing to read *A Faithful Guardian*. This story is set on a fictional ranch beside the Rio Grande near the fictional town of Riverton, New Mexico.

This book is a legacy sequel to my Love Inspired Historical novella, *Yuletide Reunion*, published in the anthology *A Western Christmas* (2015), two LIH novels, *Finding Her Frontier Family* (2022) and *Finding Her Frontier Home* (2023), and my first contemporary Love Inspired book, *Safe Haven Ranch* (2024). I started with a family of five Mattson brothers back in the 1880s. Each one found his ladylove and lived happily ever after. Now it's time to see what has happened to some of the many descendants of these fine Christian characters. Thus, in *A Faithful Guardian*, we meet modern rancher Robert Mattson V and some of his many Mattson cousins.

Of course, literary characters need settings in which to act out their stories. My original inspiration for these ranch settings beside the Rio Grande was my sister's real-life tiny ranch, yes, beside that mighty river. In my visits to her beautiful pink (and historic) adobe house, I was swept back in history and my writerly imagination got busy creating characters and stories. Thus the Mattson legacy began...and continues.

I love to hear from my readers, so if you enjoyed *A Faithful Guardian*, please write and let me know. Please also visit my website: louisemgougeauthor.blogspot.com, find me on Facebook: facebook.com/LouiseMGougeAuthor or follow me on BookBub: bookbub.com/profile/louise-m-gouge.

God bless you.
Louise M. Gouge

   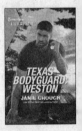

LOVE INSPIRED
INSPIRATIONAL ROMANCE

Stories to uplift and inspire

DISCOVER.

SCAN ME

Find which books are coming next month from your favorite Love Inspired authors at
LoveInspired.com/shop/pages/new-releases.html

EXPLORE.

SCAN ME

Sign up for the Love Inspired e-newsletter and download a free book at
TryLoveInspired.com

CONNECT.

Join our Love Inspired community to share your thoughts and connect with other readers!

 Facebook.com/LoveInspiredBooks
𝕏 **Twitter.com/LoveInspiredBks**

LIIBC2024R

An unexpected canine friendship
Could bring their families together

After her teen daughter, Zoey, bonds with a stray dog, the last thing Lauren Parker anticipates is the owner accusing her of stealing it. The prominent rancher and widowed father, Robert Mattson, doesn't believe Lauren's innocence, but even he can see the special understanding his dog, Lady, has for Zoey's medical needs. When Robert's twins become fast friends with Zoey, his prickly interactions with Lauren soon give way to something more. As Lady brings them all closer together, Robert can't harden his heart any longer...but is he too late to win Lauren's love?

A K-9 COMPANIONS TALE

CATEGORY: **HOPE & INSPIRATION**

$7.99 U.S./$8.99 CAN.

ISBN-13: 978-1-335-93696-7

50799

EAN

9 781335 936967

S

Uplifting stories of
faith, forgiveness and hope.

LOVE INSPIRED

LoveInspired.com

THE TEXAN'S
JOURNEY
HOME

JOLENE NAVARRO

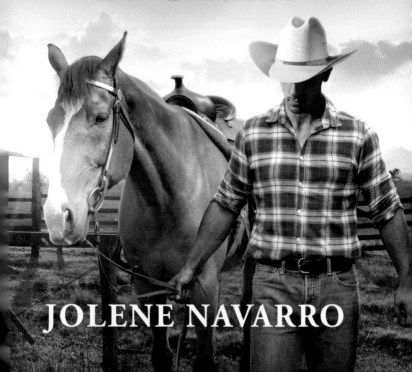

LOVE INSPIRED
INSPIRATIONAL ROMANCE

Uplifting stories of faith, forgiveness and hope.

Fall in love with stories where faith helps guide you through life's challenges, and discover the promise of a new beginning.

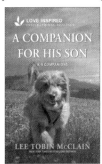

Six new books available every month!

ISBN-13: 978-1-335-93698-1

EAN

LIIFC2024R1